"Damn you, Clay..."

Erica's voice was almost a whisper. "I was fine till I met you. Why couldn't you have been a plain old cowboy who just wanted a good time—no conditions, no past, no future, nothing but the pleasure of the moment?"

Clay grinned as he pushed a strand of hair off her cheek. "I think I've proven I can have a good time. I've got no conditions and I'm *all* for pleasure."

"That just leaves the past and the future," she murmured.

"Leave the past alone. And as for the future..." His gaze settled on her soft, inviting mouth.

"Kiss me now, please..." she demanded.

Taking her into his arms, Clay let his mouth wander over hers, nipping, teasing, tasting. His hand ran up under her shirt and over the curve of her hip to her narrow waist.

After a minute Erica came up for air. Clay smiled as he cupped her breast. He felt hard and ready. "Want to hear rule seven of the Cowboy Code?" he asked lazily.

"Okay, what's rule seven?"

"*Never* make a lady ask twice."

Laughing, she pulled his face back down to hers.

Dear Reader,

Welcome to The Cowboy Club! This legendary bar/restaurant is located in colorful Red Rock, Colorado. Locals consider The Cowboy Club the heart and soul of the town. Nearly everyone has a story to tell about the club. And *everybody* has met somebody special there....

Step into The Cowboy Club and take a seat. Experience the magic of this romantic place. Watch as strong sexy heroes encounter the kind of sassy women that make them want to give up their bachelor ways and commit.

In *Love You Forever,* Clay McCormick has given up on love after losing the most important woman in his life. Erica Ross has her own heartache. But when these two meet at The Cowboy Club, they discover that true love— and a little magic—can change everything.

Come back to The Cowboy Club in January 1999 with *The Bride Wore Boots.* Chloe James, gorgeous shoe designer from New York, finds herself the half owner of the club. Arriving in Red Rock, she plans to sell her interest and head home pronto. But Chloe's high heels prove her downfall! She slips and literally falls into the arms of hero Dax Charboneau. This sexy bad boy is her new partner—and he's got plans for Chloe *and* the club!

Hope you enjoy your visit to The Cowboy Club!

Happy reading,

Janice Kaiser

LOVE YOU FOREVER
Janice Kaiser

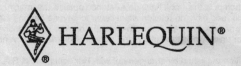

TORONTO • NEW YORK • LONDON
AMSTERDAM • PARIS • SYDNEY • HAMBURG
STOCKHOLM • ATHENS • TOKYO • MILAN • MADRID
PRAGUE • WARSAW • BUDAPEST • AUCKLAND

ISBN 0-373-25802-X

LOVE YOU FOREVER

Copyright © 1998 by Belles Lettres, Inc.

This edition published by arrangement with Harlequin Books S.A.

® and TM are trademarks of the publisher. Trademarks indicated with
® are registered in the United States Patent and Trademark Office, the
Canadian Trade Marks Office and in other countries.

Printed in U.S.A.

1

SHE HAD BEEN DRIVING for nearly nine hours—not counting her lunch in Grand Junction—and hadn't seen so much as a service station in fifty miles. She was tired, but figured she must be close. The entrance to the ranch couldn't be far.

When another jackrabbit hopped out of the sagebrush and onto the road, Erica tooted the horn. To her great relief, the rabbit scampered off. It must have been the fifth or sixth one. Rabbits and circling hawks were about the only life she'd seen since she'd turned onto this secondary road half an hour earlier. Where were all the cows? This was cattle country, wasn't it?

Erica Ross knew very little about ranches or ranching, though she'd lived in Colorado her entire life. This southwestern part of the state was desolate in comparison to Denver, or even Colorado Springs where she'd grown up. The greener, pine-covered mountains had given way to more arid, sage-studded plateaus and barren buttes and peaks. It was rough, primitive country. And hot. Erica was grateful for the air-conditioning. Her Ford Escort was old and she never knew when the air-conditioning, or even the engine, might give out. But it was what she could afford. And if she wanted to work, she had no choice but to travel to where she could find a suitable position.

Sally Nobel, her best friend, thought she was nuts to take the job. "A month with cows and coyotes and snakes, Erica? You'll go bonkers!"

"The snakes are not the attraction, believe me," she'd told Sally.

"Then what is? Besides the money, of course."

"The money."

Sally laughed.

"Well, there're always the cowboys," Erica added slyly.

"*You* and a cowboy?"

She made a face. "Probably not, now that I think about it. I've never known one. A real one, I mean. Have you?"

Sally hadn't, but said she didn't need to to know she'd be bored. Erica agreed that a month around guys who got their kicks out of pressing hot pokers to the butts of cows could be a long time. But the project wasn't exactly about cowboys. It was about a ghost-town theme park, and that could be very interesting. That she'd be working on a ranch was incidental. At least, that's what she told herself.

Sally, always the skeptic, had wondered if Tom didn't have something to do with her taking on this project. Sally had been with her when they ran into Tom Brandon at the Web Site, the hot dance club in south Denver, a few weeks earlier. He had been with his new fiancée, a bosomy redhead whose name Erica didn't catch. It was the first time she'd seen him since he'd broken their engagement a year and a half ago.

"Did you see her ring?" Sally exclaimed the second Tom and Boobsie had gone off. "That was *your* ring!"

"It wasn't *my* ring, Sally. It was Tom's. He recycled it, that's all."

"You never should have given it back to him. The bastard."

Sally had been more bitter about Tom breaking off the engagement than Erica had been—though Erica knew in her heart of hearts that it had hurt plenty at the time. But she'd found out the kind of man Tom was, which was lucky. Better that than to find out after she married the guy that he was a heartless bastard.

Actually, that wasn't fair. Tom wasn't a bastard; he was weak. Weak and scared and selfish, though maybe the selfish part could be forgiven. What guy in his right mind would want to marry a woman who had hepatitis C? The disease was the real villain.

"If he loved you enough, it wouldn't have mattered," Sally had said at the time.

Erica knew that was probably true. And a big part of her wanted to believe that some man—the right man—would love her so much, nothing would keep him from marrying her. But she'd come to realize that was unrealistic. Why should any man take damaged goods if he didn't have to? It was one thing if your spouse got sick, another thing entirely to marry someone who already had an incurable, potentially fatal disease. What kind of life would Tom, or any other guy, have had to look forward to under those conditions?

Besides which, given the circumstances, she had decided that there was no way she could have kids.

Nor would she adopt since there was a chance that she might leave some poor innocent child motherless. Was that fair to Tom? To any guy?

So she'd forgiven Tom. And convinced herself that, if nothing else, he'd helped her to see that relationships—permanent ones anyway—would be a problem for her down the line. The good news, and the bottom line, as far as she was concerned, was that her life wasn't over. To the contrary, her illness had liberated her. Sure, she was fragile, and there was always a chance she might get really sick and die, but it was also possible she'd live a fairly normal life, assuming she was careful and took precautions, especially to avoid stress.

Determined not to let Tom's rejection get her down, she'd dated other men in the last year or so, though none of the relationships had been serious. She no longer wanted anything serious, because that simply wasn't in the cards.

And yet, when she saw Tom and his new fiancée that night, she felt a twinge of regret...and pain. Did that mean she'd taken the job in Red Rock to get away? Erica didn't think so. Sure, she welcomed a change of scene. Maybe there would even be a chance for a little fun in Red Rock, despite the snakes. The cowboys would surely be boring in the long run, but she was talking a month out here. How bad could it be?

Another reason she'd decided to take the job was that she liked Julia Sommers—at least, she liked her over the phone. The elderly woman sounded like a real hoot. "Be warned, Miss Ross," she'd said as they'd negotiated the terms of Erica's contract. "You'll be walking into a hornet's nest. There are folks who will think I'm nuts trying to build a theme park in the middle of nowhere, people who will do whatever they can to stop me. But I've also got friends, and I've got history on my side."

Erica wasn't sure what Mrs. Sommers had meant by history, but she was certain to find out soon enough. She was aware that Julia had been a Hollywood actress who had come to Red Rock back in the days when it had been a mecca for filming westerns. Julia had made three pictures before giving up acting for the love of her life—a local rancher. After her marriage, she'd successfully operated the Cowboy Club.

When Erica had first heard Julia mention the Cowboy Club, she was struck by the name. Instantly her imagination conjured up a colorful Old West saloon. She could almost envision John Wayne or Glenn Ford striding in to ask for a whiskey, straight up. And after reading the materials Julia had sent her about the town, Erica realized she hadn't been far off the mark. The club had been the premier watering hole and restaurant in Red Rock for decades. It was a favorite with locals, not to mention the actors and directors and film crews of a bygone era who had patronized the place.

In a way, Erica was sorry that Julia wasn't hiring her to consult about the Cowboy Club; the place sounded fascinating. The idea of a ghost town had also captured her imagination though. Of course, it wasn't a real ghost town, but the remains of a film set that had been abandoned years earlier. Julia owned the land on which the set had been built, and she was thinking of turning it into a theme park, capitalizing on the history of Red Rock. Erica's job would be to analyze the plan and determine if the idea was feasible.

Erica checked the odometer again. Unfortunately she'd neglected to note the reading when she'd turned off of Route 184 onto this secondary road, so she couldn't be sure how much farther she had to go. Surely, though, it wasn't far. She certainly hoped not, because she was getting tired.

She had been under standing orders from her doctor not to push herself. It had been a long day, but general fatigue wasn't the main concern. Stress was the killer. That was why she'd given up her marketing job to do consulting, so that she could pick and choose projects and do them at her own pace.

She glanced out the side window at the terrain. The rocky outcroppings running parallel to the road were more ruddy than those farther north. This was harshly beautiful country. Red Rock. She was starting to understand the name.

Coming over a rise, Erica saw a long, straight stretch of road ahead, the asphalt surface shimmering in the heat waves. She could make out a large object half a mile or so away at the edge of the road, but she couldn't say for sure what it was because of the refraction of the light in turbulent air. Then, at a distance of a quarter of a mile, she saw it was a pickup truck. A figure stood on the pavement beside it, a man.

When she'd closed to within a hundred yards or so, he began waving an object. Her first assumption was that it was a flag and that he was signaling her to stop. Wary, she slowed, wondering if there'd been an accident. But it was soon apparent that the man simply wanted a lift. The object in his hand was a gas can.

Erica was torn. Should she stop and give the stranger a ride, or continue on? She knew darned well no woman in her right mind would stop for a hitchhiker in an isolated spot. Even if he did need help, there was no telling what might enter his mind once he was in her car. No, he'd have to get a lift from somebody else.

Moving to the far side of the road to pass him, she went by at about thirty miles an hour, slow enough to see disappointment registered on his face. And disbelief. The man was a cowboy in boots, hat, jeans and a sweaty, faded blue work shirt. The pickup was a rusty old wreck, which told her all she needed to know. She could almost hear Sally laughing. "Hey, what was wrong with that one? He was kind of cute. Bet he can really square-dance!"

Apparently the cowboy thought he merited a helping hand because when she glanced in the rear-view mirror she saw him glaring in utter exasperation, his hands on his hips. Erica felt badly, but what could she do? Compassion was all well and good, but common sense was what kept a smart woman from harm's way. Someone else would have to be the Good Samaritan.

Then she recalled that there hadn't been any traffic since she'd left 184. The poor man could be there for hours. It was hot. He might have important business somewhere. Maybe he was headed into town to get groceries for his family.

Erica pulled off the pavement. She checked the rearview mirror. The truck was again a small blur, shimmering in the heat waves half a mile back. She couldn't see the cowboy. Balancing the danger against the good she might do, she wondered if she dared go back. She could at least satisfy herself that he hadn't been bitten by a rattlesnake or something.

Even knowing it was more out of fear of being heartless than genuine courage, she turned the car around and headed back. As she neared the truck, the cowboy climbed out of the cab, where he'd taken refuge from the sun. By the time she reached him, he was leaning against the door, his arms folded over his chest, one booted foot resting on the running board. He did not move, even when she rolled to a stop opposite him, though he did push up the brim of his hat with his index finger, revealing a sweaty but angularly handsome face. He was tall and well built and appeared to be in his mid-thirties. He had the well-tanned, rugged look of a man who spent his time outdoors.

Erica rolled the window halfway down. "What happened?"

"Put some tainted fuel in my tank," he said, giving the gas can a gentle kick.

"Are you all right?" she asked.

He shook his head slowly, a philosophical expression on his face. "Well, I've got a canteen in the truck. That water ought to keep me alive for four or five days. Haven't got any food, but don't reckon I'll starve to death before then anyway."

Erica smiled, though she wasn't sure if he was making fun of her or trying to put her at ease. "Do you live nearby?"

"Yes, ma'am. On the Lone Eagle Ranch, back up behind this mountain," he said, tossing his head.

"The Lone Eagle Ranch?"

"You know it?"

"Not really, but that's where I'm headed."

He seemed surprised and at the same time intrigued. "That a fact?" he said, straightening his lanky body. "You're headed exactly where I need to go. I don't suppose I could talk you into giving me a lift."

Erica shook her head. "No, I'm afraid I can't help you that way."

"Ma'am?"

"I said, I can't give you a ride. I have a policy never to pick up strange men on the highway."

He rolled his tongue around in his cheek, his eyes twinkling. "I don't rightly regard myself as strange, ma'am. In fact, I'm entirely normal. Ask anybody."

"Well, obviously, there's no one to ask but you, and you're not exactly objective."

He grinned. "It appears we have a problem."

"No, *I* don't have a problem. *You* do, sorry to say."

"Then what in the hell did you come back for?" he said with a frown.

"I wanted to make sure you weren't in immediate danger."

"Well, I could fall down on the pavement and writhe around a little, if that would get me a ride," he teased.

"Look, I don't consider this a joking matter. I'm trying to be humane without being stupid."

"I see," he said, mock seriously. "Wouldn't want you to feel badly about yourself. That would be a real tragedy. So don't you worry a bit. I'll be okay here. Meditating on the sagebrush is a kind of therapy. I do it often. You go on about your business now and have a nice day."

He was goading her, which annoyed her a little, but Erica could hardly blame him. She wasn't helping him and she was embarrassing herself. It was worse than if she'd kept going. Still, she couldn't forget that only last year there was a college student in Denver who picked up girls in singles' bars, then raped and murdered them. Five women. He was good-looking and, according to the article in the *Denver Post*, charming as hell. Erica knew better than to give in to temptation.

"I admit I'm paranoid," she said. "But with good reason. Just tell me if there's something I can do short of letting you in the car."

"Well, if you'd tell one of the boys at the ranch that Clay McCormick's sitting out on the highway with tainted gas and needs to be picked up, I'd be much obliged. Tell 'em I'm about five miles west of the entrance to the ranch. They'll find me."

"Gladly, Mr. McCormick."

"Thank you, ma'am."

He smiled as if to say "no hard feelings" then saluted her by touching two fingers to the brim of his hat.

Erica nodded back.

"Oh, there is one thing," he said.

"Yes?"

He slowly ambled toward the car. Erica rolled up the window all but a crack, eliciting a slight smile from him.

He leaned on the door, peering in at her with gray wolflike eyes, his wide mouth amused. "You might want to be careful," he said, growing serious.

"There's a place on the ranch road about a mile or so from the highway where you go up a narrow draw. Be real vigilant when you drive through that stretch. It's an ideal place for an ambush and the Apache have been known to waylay a lone vehicle."

"Indians?" she said, a little surprised.

"There's maybe half a dozen renegades, that's all. It's not like a whole tribe or anything. They've been roaming the hills east of here for three, four years now, looking for easy prey. The sheriff's gone looking for them a hundred times, but they're slippery devils. Fact is, they aren't all that dangerous... Haven't killed anybody in a long time now, so you probably don't have much to fear. But it's best knowing what you're up against."

"Are you serious?" Erica said.

"Ma'am, do I look like somebody who'd spin a yarn?"

She stared at him for several moments, trying to discern his intent, when a broad smile broke over his handsome mouth and she realized he *was* kidding her. She shook her head with disgust. "That's not at all funny, Mr. McCormick."

"Maybe not. But I did have you goin' there for a minute, didn't I?" he said, chuckling.

"Is that what you do for sport around here, have fun with gullible women?"

His eyes twinkled. "I kind of thought you deserved it."

"You're shaming me," she said.

"No, ma'am. If you want the honest truth, I'm trying to charm you into trusting me so I won't have to sit out here any longer than necessary. I've had all my shots. No rabies, no mad cow disease. Haven't

even had a cold in two years. About the worst thing
you can say about me is I've got a little cow manure
on the edge of my boots. But it's dry and you get
used to the smell soon enough."

She shook her head, amused, though she hated to
admit it. Clay McCormick was trying to manipulate
her, he'd confessed to it. The irony was, the longer
she talked to him, the more foolish her caution
seemed. In truth, she was starting to feel like an id-
iot. And when she looked into his gray eyes, she realized, though probably not as quickly as he, that
her resistance was breaking down.

"I don't suppose you have any identification,"
she said, trying, despite herself, to sound reasonable
and at the same time maintain her dignity.

"Indeed I do."

Reaching into his hip pocket, Clay produced a
badly worn leather wallet, which he opened. Then,
removing his driver's license, he pressed it to the
window. Erica gazed at the grinning image of a
happy-go-lucky cowboy. His name was on the license, "Clay McCormick," together with a Red Rock
rural-route address.

"All right, I'll give you a lift to the ranch," she
said. "I wouldn't want your dying of sunstroke on
my conscience."

Clay peered at her through the crack in the window. "You sure?"

"Yes."

He seemed pleased, but he took off his hat and
scratched his head. "I hate to tell you this, but I'll
have to take my rifle. It'd be irresponsible to leave it
in the truck. And it could come in handy if we have
a run-in with those renegades," he said with a wink.

She groaned, seeing he'd worked her into a corner. "Okay, fine, get the rifle."

Clay got it from the gun rack in the rear window of the pickup. Moving swiftly, he returned to the car, opened the door, which she'd unlocked, and stuck the rifle on the boxes in the back seat. Then he removed his sweat-stained hat and plopped down beside her, his large, angular frame filling the small space. He had a couple of days' growth of beard on his jaw and smelled of leather and sage and sweat. She didn't notice the scent of manure, but that might have been part of the mix as well.

"Sorry it's so crowded," she said.

"Hey, beggars can't be choosers," he said, resting his hat on his knee. "I appreciate you taking a chance. I know it wasn't easy."

"Let's hope you prove it was the right thing to do."

"You haven't a thing to worry about, I promise you," he said. "But I'm curious, why did you want to see my ID? Criminals have driver's licenses, too, you know. I mean, I wasn't asking you to cash a check or anything."

She blushed, knowing he had her. "You're right, of course," she said, putting the car in gear and starting down the road. "It just…felt better, I guess…knowing you weren't a pathological liar."

"If you're referring to my little joke, the fact of the matter is there has been some trouble on the ranch with renegades."

"Really? Or are you trying to get me a second time?" she said warily.

"Nope. I'm telling the truth." He chuckled. "But

the last incident was back in 1913, so the prospects of me having to use my rifle are slim.''

"Thank goodness for small favors," she said, keeping her eye on the road.

Clay McCormick wasn't watching the road, though. He was watching her. And that made Erica uncomfortable. Admittedly, the man had a certain rustic charm, but she wasn't going to embrace him like an old friend, or for that matter a new one. She was still half-afraid letting him in the car had been a dreadful mistake.

"So," he said after a while, "you have a name, I bet, or is that something you city girls don't give out till the second date?"

"Is it my imagination, Mr. McCormick, or do you have something against people from the city?"

"I best not answer that, ma'am, or you'll stop the car and make me get out."

"That bad, huh?"

"No, I guess I'm teasing you. Cities are okay. I visit them from time to time, but I'm basically a man of the land. I love my life out here and wouldn't trade it for all the stock in IBM."

"My name's Erica Ross."

"Nice to meet you, Miss Ross…or may I call you Erica?"

"Erica's fine."

Clay McCormick drummed his fingers on the door handle as he glanced into the back seat. "I know I sound like I'm full of questions," he said, "but I'm mighty curious about why you're headed to the Lone Eagle."

"I'm calling on Mrs. Sommers," she said obliquely.

He hesitated. "You're right. It isn't any of my business."

Erica decided not to comment. It *wasn't* any of his business.

"I suppose I shouldn't ask what you do in Denver either," he said.

"How did you—"

"License-plate frame."

"Oh," she said. "I'm a business consultant, Mr. McCormick."

"With a résumé like that, you best call me Clay."

She laughed. "How about you? What do you do at the Lone Eagle Ranch? Are you a ranch hand?"

"You can always tell by the smell," he said with a grin. "'Hang around cows and you end up smelling like 'em.' That's rule number seventeen of the Cowboy Code, by the way."

"Cowboy Code?"

"Yep, we have a code we live by, ma'am. It's not written, mind you, but every cowpoke and buckaroo west of the Mississippi carries it in his head. Damn near as important to survival as having a good horse."

"I must remember that."

She could feel his eyes again and glanced over at him. He wore a smile, his manner extremely self-confident. He was definitely flirting, probably because there weren't any available women on the ranch and it was still a while before Saturday rolled around. Maybe he even had designs on her, figuring he could get a shot in before the other hands found out she was there.

Erica could hear Sally chuckling all the way from Denver. "Lassoed before you even got out of the car, eh, cowgirl?'' Well, Clay McCormick was cute all right, but at the ripe old age of twenty-nine, Erica had grown beyond getting bowled over by a good-looking guy. If anything, his novelty value had more appeal than his looks, but she had no intention of encouraging him. She was, after all, a professional and she was here to do a job, not to discover the wonders of the cowboy culture up close and personal.

She decided to divert him with conversation. ''Do you know Mrs. Sommers well, Clay?''

''I guess you could say that. I live on the same ranch. But the fact is, everybody in the county knows Julia. She's quite a gal.''

''Is she? We've never met. To this point, we've only corresponded and spoken on the phone.''

''Then you're in for a real treat,'' he said. ''She's as colorful a figure as you'll find in these parts. Virtually a legend.''

''Because of the Cowboy Club?'' she asked, turning to him.

He blinked. ''You know about that?''

''She mentioned it and there were a number of references in the materials I got from the chamber of commerce,'' Erica replied. ''Sounds like the club was an important part of her life. She ran it for a number of years, didn't she?''

''Until she sold her interest to Dax Charboneau a while back, yeah.''

Erica noticed a discernible change in Clay's tone. ''Was that good or bad?''

''I reckon it depends entirely on your point of view.''

''What's your opinion?''

Clay took a deep breath. "I don't know if there's any point in stirring up that pot."

"A sensitive issue, is it?" she asked.

"Well, the town's of two minds on what the future of Red Rock should be. Some folks would like to see things stay pretty much as they are and others think we're sitting on a mound of gold that ought to be mined. The Cowboy Club sits in the middle of the controversy—mostly because the people associated with it, including Julia, are the so-called progressives who want to turn Red Rock into a tourist town."

"I take it you're opposed to the idea."

He grinned at her. "I'm a traditionalist and I guess it shows."

"What's so bad about the Cowboy Club, anyway?"

"Not a thing," Clay replied. "Back in the days when they shot westerns in Red Rock, the film stars hung out there. Locals and actors both hung out at the place, made it their home away from home. Lots of romances started there. Julia even met her husband there...which may explain why she's so partial to it. When she ran the place, she capitalized on the past, especially the Hollywood connection. It sort of added to the lore, I guess. But I say leave it in the past. We don't need to attract carloads of tourists here just to make a buck. In my opinion, cattle country is for cattlemen. Not for citified dandies selling macramé, California art, postcards and souvenirs made in China."

"Sounds like I've struck a nerve," she said.

"'New and improved can't beat tried-and-true.'"

"More Cowboy Code?"

"Rule five."

"Seems I've got a lot to learn," she said.

"I don't mean to drag you into our little squabbles before you've had a chance to climb down from your horse, Erica. I'm sure Julia will be giving you the other side of the story."

She couldn't help wondering if he had any idea what brought her to Red Rock—not that the opinion of one cowhand would matter all that much to Julia Sommers or, for that matter, anyone else. But if somebody like Clay McCormick got this hot under the collar about the subject, Erica could only imagine how it was when the town's movers and shakers got together.

For a ranch hand, the guy seemed rather astute. But then, maybe she had been expecting too little. She'd never known any real cowboys. Most of the men tromping around Denver in braided shirts and shiny boots were "all hat and no horse." Clay McCormick seemed the genuine article.

He certainly had opinions. He also had a sense of humor and a certain...appeal. She imagined there were hundreds of Clay McCormicks in western Colorado, though surely not many quite as sexy.

"The entrance to the ranch is just over the next rise," he said, breaking her train of thought. "On your left."

Erica slowed as they went over the rise. There was a large arched sign and when she got close she could see it read Lone Eagle Ranch. She'd come a long way, but she'd made it. "At long last," she said.

"Now all we have to do is get past the badlands and the Apache," he said.

"Fortunately I've got you for protection," she said wryly.

"Kind of like the sound of that, Erica," he said with a slow smile. "Kind of do."

2

THEY'D CROSSED over the ridge and come down into the valley where the ranch house and other buildings were located. The surrounding pastureland was irrigated and green. Erica thought it rather pretty.

They'd joked about the Apache, but Clay told her how just after the turn of the century a war party had harassed some of the local ranches, including the Lone Eagle. Had it not been for the presence of some extra hands hired for the roundup, it could have been a disaster. "Turned out they drove the Indians off, shot one of them," he said, "I guess bringing the end of an era. The stuff of local legend."

"Would you have liked to have been around then?" she asked.

"Not for the killing part, no. But my people go way back and I feel connected to the land. I wouldn't have minded being in my great-great-grandfather's shoes, one of the first to settle this country."

Erica detected pride in his voice. Clay McCormick was indeed a traditionalist, as he had said. It wasn't that often you met a real throwback. She could only imagine what he must think of her, a greenhorn, dropping in out of nowhere.

They approached the hillock where the main

house was located. "You can go on up the driveway to the ranch house," Clay said, gesturing.

Erica did as he said, following the driveway along the sweep of lawn toward the low, rambling stone building with a deep porch covered with vines. There was an abundance of flowers in surrounding beds. The structure appeared substantial, but it had a warmth and hominess.

After stopping the engine, Erica turned to Clay. "Thanks for directing me," she said, expecting him to clamber out and head to the bunkhouse. "And I'm sorry if I gave you a bad time about the lift."

"Say nothing of it," he said, opening the door. "We make allowances for city folk."

He gave her that wry, amused smile. It was hard to tell if he was still having fun at her expense or if it was good-natured teasing. Erica climbed out, stretching her stiff legs. She walked around the car where Clay waited, holding his rifle. Offering her hand, she said, "It was really nice meeting you."

"No need to say goodbye just yet," he replied. "I'll take you in and introduce you."

She was surprised by that. But then, maybe the hands had the run of the place. Erica got her purse and briefcase from the back seat and went with him along the short stone walk to the porch. Clay opened the heavy wooden door without knocking. She stepped into the cool flagstone entry.

A Mexican woman of about forty, a housekeeper by appearances, came to greet them. "Señor McCormick," she said. "You're late."

"I was held up, Rosita," he said, tossing his hat on a chair. "This is Erica Ross. She's come to see Julia."

"Welcome, *señorita*," the smiling, round-faced woman said. "We are expecting you."

"Thank you." Erica was still trying to understand Clay's behavior and the deference he was being shown. Had she made some invalid assumptions?

"Where is Julia?" Clay asked the housekeeper.

"In the sunroom, *señor*."

He leaned his rifle against the wall and took Erica's arm. "Right this way," he said.

They walked through the rambling house to a large glass-enclosed room in back. It was cheerful and bright and nicely furnished with plush chairs and a fat sofa in a beige the shade of sagebrush. On the walls were bold paintings in earth tones. The mood was strongly southwestern. Seated in the far corner in a large highback chair was a little white-haired woman in her late seventies. She wore a bright blue caftan, heavy gold jewelry and glasses.

"Gram, you've got a visitor," Clay said, drawing the woman's eyes up from the book she was reading.

Erica gave Clay a double take as he led her across the room. The woman had put aside her book and got to her feet.

"You must be Erica," she said, greeting her warmly. "I'm Julia Sommers."

"Hello, Mrs. Sommers," she said, still unnerved by her apparent misunderstanding of Clay's identity. So he and Julia were related?

"Clay," Julia scolded, "you look like you just got off your horse. What are you doing tramping around the house that way?" She peered down at his boots.

"Sorry, Gram," he replied. "I was stuck out on the

highway. Truck broke down. Erica gave me a lift to the ranch."

"I'm surprised she'd help you out, looking the way you do."

"She very nearly didn't," he said, giving Erica a wink.

She had to close her mouth. "You're her grandson?"

He grinned.

"You didn't tell her, Clay?" Julia said.

"Why prejudice her thinking, Gram?"

"Knowing you, young man," Julia said, wagging her finger, "prejudice her thinking is exactly what you tried to do!"

He laughed.

Erica thought of how he'd sort of led her down the primrose path—acting innocent, asking questions— and she was annoyed.

Clay must have seen her feelings in her eyes because he said, "You didn't exactly ask me who I was and I didn't exactly lie in response to any questions."

She gave him a rueful look. "Perhaps. But you let me assume certain things."

"That wasn't my intent."

"Did you know who I was and why I'm here?" she asked.

Clay glanced at Julia. "Gram and I are close, but she doesn't tell me all her business and I don't tell her all mine. So, no, I don't know what, exactly, you're here for," he said.

"Clay McCormick," Julia said, her tone more pointed, "were you trying to weasel information out of this young lady?"

"No, Mrs. Sommers," Erica said, answering for him. "That wasn't the problem. He did mislead me though."

"That's nearly as bad," Julia said.

She was still a beautiful woman with her grandson's gray eyes and the classic bone structure that had probably made her a real beauty half a century earlier. And she had a warmth that Erica found appealing.

"Look, if I've offended either of you, I apologize," Clay said. "Frankly, Erica, I was more interested in the fact that you were coming to the Lone Eagle at all, than what your business was. We don't get visitors of your ilk all that often."

"You may be smart to quit while you're ahead, Clay," Julia said. "No harm seems to be done, so why don't you skedaddle? And for heaven's sake, get cleaned up!"

"Gram, if you'd told me your guest was going to be a pretty gal, I'd have put on my Sunday best. Before I make myself presentable, though, I will have to tend to my truck and do a couple of other chores."

"I don't know why you keep that contraption," Julia said. "It's the most disreputable thing on this ranch."

"You know I've got sentimental attachments to anything and everything that belonged to my daddy."

Julia shrugged. "Who am I to question that? You go on now and let Erica and me be."

"Afternoon, then, ladies." He gave Erica another wink. "See you later." Then he left.

Erica and Julia both looked after him.

"That boy is a rascal," Julia said when he'd disappeared from sight. "I hope he didn't give you too bad a time."

"No, I guess I was a victim of my own naiveté. I assumed he was just a ranch hand."

"Clay likes to tease, there's no denying that." Julia drew her toward one of the fat sofas. They both sat. "But he's my flesh and blood and I love him. My daughter Mimi's boy. She passed away twenty years ago when Clay was just a teenager. They were close and her death devastated him." Julia smoothed her caftan. "Clay lost his dad, Mimi's husband, Wade, a couple of years ago. Another blow. Most of the Lone Eagle is his now, making him one of the richest men in western Colorado."

"Incredible."

"You won't hear him bragging about it," Julia said. "The boy's not full of himself...at least when it comes to his wealth. He does have some contrary ideas, however."

"He led me to believe he didn't fully agree with your plans for Red Rock."

"Ha! That's an understatement, if ever I heard one." Julia chortled. "In his eyes, about the only thing I did right, businesswise, was sell my interest in the Cowboy Club. When Clay was a little tyke, I used to sing at the club on Friday and Saturday nights. Mimi and Wade took him and his sister to hear me a time or two and Mimi said Clay used to get so embarrassed seeing his gram belting out love songs that he'd hide his face." Julia laughed. "I'm sure he'd still blush if I was crazy enough to hobble up on stage again."

"I don't suppose many young cowpokes could

claim to have a grandmother like you," Erica said as they exchanged smiles.

"Claim or disclaim. Now his sister, Kiley, couldn't be more different. She's off in London, studying drama. A child after my own heart."

"You must be pleased, considering your background as an actress."

"I wasn't much of an actress, dear. Would-be starlet, at best, and I knew it. All I needed was one look at Hap Sommers and my career ended." Julia got a naughty look in her eye and leaned conspiratorially toward Erica. "If you ever want to get Clay's goat, remind him that he's got Hollywood blood in his veins!" She laughed and slapped her leg. "Mostly we tease about it, but he's dead set against turning Red Rock into a tourist town, even if it means money and jobs for a lot of people. 'New and improved can't beat tried-and-true,' is the way he puts it."

"Rule five of the Cowboy Code, if I'm not mistaken," Erica said with a grin.

Julia rolled her eyes. "Lord, he's already been indoctrinating you."

"No, I'd say it's more a matter of him being himself."

"Clay's nothing if he's not consistent. The closer to nature he can keep things, the better. He's convinced himself that he'd be just as happy without electricity and running water, so long as he had his horse."

Erica bit the inside of her cheek to keep from giggling. "You paint quite a picture."

"The boy's no fool. And if he puts his mind to it, he can be a real gentleman, and quite charming too."

Erica saw no point in mentioning she'd already

seen his charming side. The gentleman part, maybe not yet. But then, Julia was comparing him with the breed of man that worked this rugged country—the cowboys. Erica's frame of reference was Denver and guys like Tom Brandon. Compared to the men she'd known, Clay McCormick was pretty rough around the edges.

"Well, enough about Clay," Julia said. "We've got business to discuss. I'm just dying to hear what you think the prospects are for my ghost town."

FROM HIS OFFICE in the main barn, Clay had telephoned Billy Wicks at the Conoco station in town and asked him about tainted gas in his tank. Billy told him they'd have to clean the fuel lines and drain the tank. Clay asked him to come out with his tow truck and get the sucker. Then he'd gone to where Emilio Juarez, the ranch foreman, and Roy, one of the ranch hands, were repairing a stall that had been damaged by a temperamental stallion. Clay watched Emilio trying to fit a board he'd cut into place in the rear wall of the stall.

"Who was the girl who brought you to the house, boss?" Emilio asked. "I couldn't see her too good, but she looked pretty."

"Yeah, she is. Came from Denver to work with Julia on one of her schemes. I flagged her down out on the highway."

"You're lucky she stopped."

"I know," Clay said. "City girl." It was all the explanation that was needed. The men nodded.

"So, what's she and Señora Sommers doing?" Emilio had been foreman of the Lone Eagle for fifteen years and had no compunction about asking questions. He made it his business to know everything that was going on and, being married to Rosita, he pretty well had the ranch covered, both inside and outside the main house. "The *señora's* not working on that dude-ranch idea again, is she?"

"No, thank God."

"*Dios mio.* Don't tell me it's that, that…what do you call those things? Like Disneyland and Jurassic Park."

"A theme park," Clay said.

"Yeah, the ghost-town theme park."

"I have a hunch that's exactly what this is about. Miss Ross had a computer in her car and I'll bet you a buffalo steak from the Cowboy Club she uses it to do feasibility studies."

"*What* kind of studies?" Emilio said.

"Feasibility. You know, figure out whether it's good business or bad business."

"You don't need no computer for that, boss. Turning Red Rock into a tourist trap is just plain stupid. Anybody can see that."

"Let's hope Miss Ross is as smart as you are, Emilio."

The foreman shook his head. "I can see it now, Roy here in a Mickey Mouse suit, greeting all the tourists."

"No way," Roy said. "Not me."

Clay and Emilio laughed.

"Don't worry," Clay told Roy. "As long as I'm boss of the Lone Eagle, no Mickey Mouse suits and no dude ranch. Everything stays just like it is."

"Fine by me," Emilio said.

"Me, too," Roy added.

Clay watched Emilio hammer the board into

place. But he wasn't thinking about the board, or even the conversation. His mind wandered to Erica Ross. He'd teased her, but damn if she didn't intrigue him. Hell, it was more than intrigue. He found her downright attractive.

She must have taken him for a real hayseed, but that was okay, he wasn't into pretension. On the other hand, he had left himself with a negative image to overcome. Disarming a gal was one thing, disgusting her was another. But then, what difference did it make? It wasn't as though he was taking her to the prom. No, it was best not to give her two thoughts. She was Julia's little playmate. Nothing but complications there.

"There," Emilio said, after hammering in the last nail. "Good as new." He ran his hand over the smooth surface of the board with seeming affection. Emilio was a man who took pride in doing things right.

As the men cleaned up, Clay asked himself if fraternizing with Erica Ross was really out of the question. God knows, there were few enough opportunities, given his life-style. The Lone Eagle wasn't exactly a magnet for young, attractive females. His sister was the only single one that had been around in years, and his main concern with her was keeping her separated from the men.

Clay never brought any women to the ranch for himself and had no intention of doing so. In fact, he'd made a point of keeping his social life as remote from Red Rock as he could. He'd had a few dalliances with ladies over in Durango, but even that was a little too close to home for comfort. No, when he felt the need for a tumble in the hay, he'd take a few days and go to Denver, Santa Fe, Phoenix or Las Vegas. Vegas was his favorite, because it pretty much existed for pleasure. The women were easy to find and they had no expectations. Fun was the name of the game, quick, superficial and meaningless. The last was the most important. It had to be meaningless.

So why was he having so much trouble dismissing Erica from his mind? Physical attraction? He liked her soft brown hair and pale blue eyes well enough. She was pretty and had a cute figure. She also had that quick, city-girl edge—but he suspected she had a softer feminine side, too. Their conversation had been brief, but he'd learned a lot about her from it. Initially his motive had been to charm her into giving him a lift, but somehow they'd connected despite her suspicions and his intentions. There'd been electricity. He'd felt it.

There was no point kidding himself, though. He'd had trouble with women ever since Laura had died. He was snake-bit. It didn't take a genius to see avoiding them was easier, less painful than dealing with them. True, a man needed his comforts, but that was no reason to let some gal get in his head and stir up trouble. No, if he was smart, he'd nip this right in the bud.

Emilio had gathered all his tools and put them in the wooden toolbox, handing it to Roy. Then he got to his feet. "That meet with your approval, boss?" the foreman said, gesturing toward the newly repaired stall.

"Yeah, looks great," Clay said, only half noticing. He was still wrestling with an image of Erica Ross, picturing her seated behind the wheel of her car, afraid he was going to pounce on her. He shook his head. If she only knew...

Emilio came out of the stall and the two of them walked along, with Roy following behind. Clay thrust his hands into his hip pockets.

"Would you do me a favor, amigo?" Clay said. "Mosey on up to the house and find out from Rosita what Julia and Erica are up to. See if it's that ghost-town scheme of hers. And I'd like to know if they're just going to chat about it over tea, or if all that gear Erica brought means she's planning on staying a while. But be discreet, know what I mean?"

"Sure," Emilio said. "But why not ask the *señora* yourself? Certainly she would tell you."

"Yeah, but I'd sort of like to know going in. It'll make dinner easier. To be forewarned is to be fore-armed, you know."

"You want me to go now?"

"Yeah, I'm going to work that new bay gelding a little. Seems a bit skittish with a rope swinging over his head."

"Good idea," Emilio said. "I've been meaning to ride him myself. With work he could be a first-class cutting horse."

"I've been thinking the same thing." He glanced over his shoulder. "Roy, would you mind throwing a saddle on that new bay for me and bringing him out to the corral?"

"Sure thing, boss."

As they stepped out into the sunlight, Emilio headed toward the house and Clay ambled over to the post-and-pole fence surrounding the corral. He clambered up to the top post, which afforded him a view across the valley. Most of the cattle were still out on the range, but there were several dozen head in the adjacent pasture, critters that had been brought in early for various reasons. Standing fifty yards or so away was a big black and brown *chongo*, a steer with a drooping horn, that had been dragged in a couple of weeks earlier. The steer had acted as crazy as it looked, though over the past few days it had finally tamed down some. One of the boys said that the *chongo* must have been feeding on locoweed, but Emilio said the poor beast was born loco, crow bait. Emilio wanted to put the critter down, but Clay said to give it a few weeks. He knew what it was like to be loco, crazy with pain of one kind or another.

Peering over his shoulder, he squinted in the bright sun at the house his grandfather had built back in the forties. Clay had been born in the place during a snowstorm and it had been the only real home he'd ever known. The little cabin at the far end of the valley where he and Laura had planned to live hardly qualified. The happy times they'd dreamed about no longer seemed real and God knew he didn't want to remember the painful times.

So the *house*, as everybody called his family home, was the only one he'd truly known. And now that woman from Denver was in it, talking to Julia. Worse was the prospect of her sticking around a while. He didn't need that kind of distraction. That Thanksgiving when Kiley brought home her boyfriend, Andrew, was nothing in comparison. Clay hadn't been as friendly as his sister would have liked, but how the hell did you talk to a guy whose ambition in life was owning a computer company? Like Erica, Andrew came from an alien world. Clay had been able to ignore him. But how did he ignore the likes of Erica Ross?

Fact was, there weren't many people around who understood ranch life. *Really* understood it. Even Julia, who'd lived here a lot longer than he, didn't. Of course, in most respects that didn't matter. He ran things on the Lone Eagle and everybody knew it, including Julia. She'd sold her interest to his parents years ago, except for that quarter section with the damn movie ghost town on it. Supposedly she'd wanted to keep it for sentimental reasons. Maybe that was true, but it sure was haunting him now.

About the time she sold the Cowboy Club, Julia started talking about turning the movie-set town into a tourist attraction. Clay was sure Dax had been the one egging her on. He liked Dax, but Charboneau was no cattleman. Damn riverboat gambler was a lot more like it—not so much in fact as temperament. Now the developers were starting to circle like a bunch of vultures. Erica Ross, cute as she was, was nothing more than an advance scout. Clay would bet the ranch on it.

The way things had turned out, when Julia had sold out her interest in the Cowboy Club, it hadn't been the end of her commercial activity—it had been a new beginning. As far as Clay could tell, Dax and Julia and Julia's former partner in the club, Cody James, all had the same goal—to put "Red Rock, Colorado" onto as many T-shirts as possible.

When Clay thought about it, he realized he shouldn't have been surprised. His grandmother still owned a lot of income property in town and probably half the vacant land. Dax and Cody owned pretty near the other half, which made them the three big land barons of Red Rock. Of course, the really big money was in the larger ranches, but Dax, Cody and Julia had their little fiefdom. Their headquarters was the Cowboy Club. Decisions were made there that would impact all their lives. And now Julia had added Erica Ross into the mix.

It wasn't long before Roy brought the bay out into the corral. Clay shortened the stirrups a notch before climbing into the saddle. The horse was skittish for a gelding. Probably just needed to be ridden regularly. A horse could develop a short memory if that suited his purposes. Clay had a scar or two on his body to prove that piece of wisdom.

For a couple of minutes he worked the horse in the corral to get him used to his hand. The bay was spirited, but quick to respond.

After a bit Clay got impatient to get out in the pasture so he could work the horse with the cattle. He glanced in the direction of the house. There was no sign of Emilio, so he moved closer to the gate. No sooner had he gotten outside the corral when the foreman appeared from behind the house and made his way toward the barn.

Clay walked the horse to the fence. Emilio approached at his own deliberate pace, same as he did everything. Once he got there, he pushed his hat up off his forehead so he could look up at Clay.

"Rosita says they've been talking about the old days when movies were made in Red Rock. They've also been talking about the Cowboy Club, Julia's singing and—you were right, boss—the ghost-town theme park."

"That's what I expected," Clay said. He peered back at the house. "Well, Julia's going to do what she's going to do. Doesn't mean I got to like it, though."

"Talk don't mean it's going to happen," Emilio volunteered.

"The ghost-town scheme may never get off the ground, but the day will come when Red Rock will be swarming with tourists. I've begun to resign myself to that, Emilio."

"I'm not so hot to see that happen," the foreman said, "but I kind of think it's neat that they used to make movies there. My uncle said he liked it when John Wayne was in town—the women would swoon over him. And the *vaqueros* would line up two and three deep at the bar in the Cowboy Club just to get a look at Maureen O'Hara."

"If Julia and her friends get their way, Emilio, we'll be lining up two and three deep at the bar, just to get a look at Herbie and Ethel from Chicago in their Hard Rock Café T-shirts and Bermuda shorts."

"It would be different, I guess."

"Yeah, well, what I don't like about it is the money drives out the real westerners. A guy either starts perming his hair and wearing leisure suits, or he moves on."

"This is big country, boss. They won't be building no housing tracts on your land."

"No, we're a hundred years from that, thank God. I guess I just hate to see things change at all." Clay took off his hat and wiped his forehead with the sleeve of his shirt. "Well, I've preached enough for one day. I'm going to ride some of the vinegar out of my blood."

Turning the bay, Clay broke him into a gallop and

they raced across the pasture, headed for a bunch of cattle in the far corner. A horse, some cows and a good piece of land—that's all a man needed. If only Julia could see it that way.

3

ERICA HAD a glass of tomato juice and Julia had a sherry while they waited for Clay. Erica had pretty much put him from her mind as she and Julia talked that afternoon, and she couldn't have been more pleased with the way things had gone. They had developed a good rapport. But now, with dinner coming, Erica again thought about Clay. Julia checked her watch for the third time in the past few minutes, her forehead creasing.

"Clay's normally on time, so I have no idea why he isn't here. I hope he isn't angry because of my project. If so, I do apologize, Erica. That wouldn't be fair to you, not to mention that it's rude."

"Don't worry about it," Erica replied. "Clay doesn't owe me anything."

"He owes you courtesy."

"He may think I'm interfering. This *is* his home and I sort of stand for everything he opposes."

"Fiddlesticks. He should be man enough to deal with it. I'm assuming—hoping, I guess—that his work kept him from being here, not bad manners."

They fell into silence. Then, after several more minutes, long enough for Julia to finish her second sherry, she said, "Well, enough's enough. If he can't get to the table on time, it's his loss. Let's eat."

As they had their salad, they chatted about the

project. Erica was pleased that Julia understood the process. She was a shrewd businesswoman, immediately grasping Erica's point about the financial risks. The seed money, Erica explained, would probably best be provided by Julia herself since outside capital was easier to attract in later stages. It was a risky venture, but the potential gains were enormous. One possible solution to the risk factor would be to scale down the project, develop it in phases. But at this point everything was speculative. A lot of research was required.

"I'm eager to see the site," Erica told her.

"Unfortunately it's not easy to get to, but I'll arrange it," Julia replied. "The old road that the film companies used has been washed out and Clay hasn't wanted to repair it. That's one of the problems, you see. To get to the ghost town, you have to cross over ten miles of Clay's land. My attorneys tell me that I have an implied easement since I'm landlocked and have no direct access to public roads, which means I can force the issue. Clay's not very pleased about that either."

"Land mines everywhere," Erica said.

"Precisely."

"Is he going to fight you?"

"We haven't gotten that far," Julia said. "Bringing you in is the first real step I've taken. Besides talk."

"So I'm sort of a shot across his bow."

"I wouldn't put it that way. I think Clay knows I can do as I wish with my own property," Julia said. "And the truth is, he wouldn't be affected all that much. It's more the idea of having a theme park on *his* ranch. Frankly, I think half the problem is that the place was built by Hollywood set designers. If it was a real western ghost town, Clay might not be so hostile to the notion, though he quails at the thought of having 'hordes of tourists,' as he calls them, poking around."

"Poor guy," Erica said. "Seems he was born in the wrong era."

"He should have been part of my generation and I should have been part of his."

Erica could see Julia's point, though it sounded as if Clay wouldn't have cared much for Hollywood in the thirties and forties either. Erica wasn't a particular fan of Hollywood, or into film stars, but Julia had painted a romantic picture of the period. She'd told Erica she'd been in three westerns that had been filmed in Red Rock. Her role in the second one, a notch below supporting actress, was the highpoint.

"You gave up a promising career to marry. Was that hard for you?"

"Surprisingly not."

"How'd you meet your husband? On the drive here, Clay said something about the Cowboy Club."

"That's right. That's where we met. I'd been spending my days on the set with all these pretend cowboys and then I'd go with a bunch of the girls in the cast to the Cowboy Club in the evening and there'd be all these real flesh-and-blood guys fresh off the range. Sure enough, I fell for one. Hap Sommers was one of those big, shy, soft-spoken men who was all iron inside, a real-life Jimmy Stewart. Hap sure knew how to pluck my chords. He had one of those deep velvety voices and an easy smile. We married six months after we met, during the shoot of my second film. It was during my third and last movie that I got pregnant with Mimi, Clay's mother. That was the end of life as a would-be starlet."

"Do you ever wonder what might have happened if you'd continued acting?" Erica asked.

"Not for a minute. I was never going to be big in Hollywood and I knew it. I was in love with Hap and spent the best thirty years of my life with him. And I kept busy. In fact, I liked the Cowboy Club so much, Hap bought me a half interest in it for our tenth anniversary. I'll tell you this, Erica, I was a better businesswoman than I was an actress."

"I have to admit I'm intrigued by what I've heard about the place."

"I hope you won't be disappointed. In some ways, it's just another western bar and restaurant, though perhaps a little more colorful than most. Yet there is something special about the place. Almost magical." Julia blushed. "Listen to me. No one would believe I was a hard-driving businesswoman when I go on like that...but the truth is, the Cowboy Club *is* special. It's real, authentic in every way. There is an air of romance with a capital *R* about it.

"I liked the club from the start," she went on, "and really came to love it—like most everyone who sets foot in the place, I guess. Lord knows, it's been a big part of my life, especially since Hap died. The club was sort of my alter ego. Some folks called me the Miss Kitty of Red Rock because of it."

"I like that image."

"I shouldn't make so much of myself," Julia said, sitting up a bit straighter. "Most folks would say the real magic is from the people who hung out there— people like John Wayne, Glenn Ford, Maureen O'Hara, Jimmy Stewart and Randolph Scott. Errol

Flynn made one movie in Red Rock, with Virginia Mayo. I wasn't in that one, but Hap and I had dinner with the two of them one night.

"The Hollywood bunch, which included me in the beginning, enjoyed the Cowboy Club because it was real, sort of like if our movies came to life." Julia smiled wistfully. "You know, Erica, they say film is magic. But for my money, the real magic was in that club. Still is. After all, I fell in love with my man there."

Erica was touched by the sentiment. And more intrigued than ever by the club. "Has it changed much since you sold your interest?"

"If anything, it might be even better," Julia said. "Dax Charboneau has brought new energy and some capital to the operation. But he has way too many irons in the fire to give the club the attention it needs. Which would be fine, except that Cody, his partner—my former partner—is getting along in years and his health isn't the best. I'd like to see new blood get interested in the place. Which is another reason I'm sorry Clay's so set in his ways. I'd never second-guess the way he ranches, but I'd like to see him expand his horizons, get involved in things apart from this ranch. Hell will probably freeze over first, but there's no harm in me wishing, I suppose."

"I can tell how important he is to you."

"He and Kiley are all I've got in the way of family, dear. God knows, there aren't any great-grand-children on the horizon."

"Your granddaughter is single, too."

"She's in love with the stage. There have been men in her life, but she's still young to be settling down anyway."

"And Clay's too busy ranching to start a family."

Julia hooted. "That boy hasn't had a decent social life since he lost Laura. At least, decent by my standards."

"Oh?"

"Laura was the girl he was engaged to years and years ago. Daughter of one of the nearby ranchers," Julia told her. "They went together in high school and were going to get married after Clay finished college. He went off and wasn't gone a year before Laura contracted leukemia. Clay came home, was with her every minute for three months until she died in his arms. He never went back to college. Instead of Laura, he married this ranch."

Julia's poignant story gave Erica a whole new perspective on Clay McCormick. "How sad. Tragic."

"The poor boy lost both parents relatively young and the girl he planned to marry. That's a lot. I've done my best to be supportive, tried to get him out of his shell, but he's stubborn and won't listen."

"Some things a person just has to deal with on their own."

"True," Julia said with a twinkle in her eye. "But I've got a stubborn streak in me, as well. I haven't given up."

"You can lead a horse to water..."

Julia observed her silently as she sipped the last of her sherry. "Erica, I was thinking I might ask Clay to take you into Red Rock, show you around. The town will certainly affect the success of my theme park, don't you think?"

"Absolutely," Erica replied. "But why ask Clay to take me? Where he's concerned, I imagine I'm about as welcome as a sheep in cattle country."

Julia smiled benevolently. "Perhaps. But I have a hunch it would be good for him."

Erica could see the wheels turning and knew exactly what Julia had in mind. She was flattered, even a little intrigued, but Lord knew, she wasn't a very good candidate for curing someone with relationship ills—she had problems of her own.

"Or am I out of line suggesting it?" Julia asked, perhaps reading the anxiety on her face. "Maybe you've got a young man and have no interest in coaxing another out of his shell."

"No, Julia, it's not that. It's just that..."

"She's not all that fond of cow manure, Gram. Don't you see baby-sitting me is the last thing she'd want?" It was Clay, standing in the doorway, wearing a western dress shirt, clean jeans and snakeskin boots. His dark hair was wet, as though he'd taken a quick shower. "Sorry I'm late for dinner, by the way," he said, ambling to the table and taking a seat. "Had some problems with the stock out by that new well and it took longer to tend to it than I thought."

Both Erica and Julia were shocked by his presence, especially considering what they'd been discussing.

"How long were you standing there, listening to our conversation, Clay McCormick?" Julia said.

"Just came up when you said you were going to ask me to take Erica into Red Rock to show her around."

"Are you sure?"

"Cross my heart," he said, giving Erica a knowing grin. He spread his napkin over his lap. "Why? Did I miss something really juicy?"

"If you had any social graces at all, you'd have

made your presence known immediately," Julia huffed.

"And miss the conspiring?"

"We were *not* conspiring!" Julia said emphatically. "I simply thought it would do you good to spend some time in the company of a refined, intelligent young woman."

"To what end, Gram?"

Erica noticed the little smile playing at the corners of his mouth and decided he was enjoying making his grandmother squirm. She was glad she hadn't said anything embarrassing.

Julia cleared her throat. "In hopes that a little of it might rub off on you, dear."

"All right," Clay declared. "I'll buy that. God knows I could use a little work in the social-graces department. One of the boys pointed out just the other day I was drawing my soup spoon toward me when I ate instead of dipping it away."

"There's no point if you're going to make light of me, young man."

"Gram, I apologize."

"It's Erica you owe the apology."

"Erica," he said, turning to her, "I regret any embarrassment I may have caused. Would you be so kind as to accept my invitation to accompany me to Red Rock tomorrow?"

"Thank you, Clay," she replied, "but the last thing I want to be is a burden. I'm sure you have much more important things to do."

"Actually, I was thinking of running into town tomorrow anyway." He lowered his voice and, in a theatrical tone, said, "You see, if you accept my invitation, I can get Gram off my back. She'll think I'm off getting gentrified, when both you and I know the best we can hope for is that you get to see Red Rock and I get to take care of business."

"Hard to resist when you put it that way," Erica said, winking at Julia.

The old woman was obviously pleased, but was avoiding showing it. She cleared her throat again. "Clay, I told Erica you were a gentleman and I very much appreciate you not proving me wrong, I really do."

"Gram, for you I'd do almost anything."

"*Almost* anything," Julia said. "Yes, I believe that, dear. For the moment, that will do nicely. Now, shall we finish our meal? Clay, eat your salad while Rosita serves the main course." Julia picked up the little bell on the table beside her and gave it a jingle.

As Clay dug into his salad, Erica tried to decide who'd won and who'd lost. It seemed Julia had gotten Clay to take her into town, which Erica could live with if she'd interpreted Clay's intentions correctly—he had things to do in Red Rock himself, which meant he had no expectations.

Julia astutely changed the subject, asking about the problem with the well. Clay told her what he'd been doing, but Erica wasn't listening closely. She was more aware of the man himself, and how different he seemed from that afternoon when she thought him an ordinary cowboy. Both his image and manner had changed, though he still had the same rustic charm, if a bit more polished.

He was definitely a hunk. The herbal cologne was nice. She liked the clean-shaven jaw, the easy, confident way he moved his body—and the feeling she got when he looked at her. It flustered her, though she did her best not to let it show.

Rosita arrived with the main course, placing a platter of roast beef on the table, along with bowls of whipped potatoes, green beans and biscuits. By the time Julia and Erica had served themselves, Clay had finished his salad, handing his plate to Rosita. He heaped whipped potatoes onto his plate. Suddenly aware she and Julia were watching him, he slowed down and put the serving spoon carefully into the bowl.

"So, did you ladies have a good afternoon?"

"A very good afternoon," Julia said, not hesitating to answer for them. "I suppose you're aware of the reason Erica's here."

"I reckon it's about your ghost town, Gram. Erica's probably your advance scout."

"She's doing a feasibility study for me, yes. I thought it best to be completely up front about it," Julia said.

"I have my opinions about that project, and I think you know what they are." He turned to Erica. "But I am capable of being civilized. If I see a role for myself in this, it's as the loyal opposition."

"I certainly don't want to be anyone's enemy," Erica said, growing uncomfortable again. The last thing she wanted was to get in the middle of a family squabble.

"No need to worry. I fraternize with friend and foe alike. Point is, you can count on my being civil."

"Thank you, dear," Julia said. "I told Erica you were a gentleman and you've proven me right."

"Boy, now the pressure's really on," he said with a laugh. "But, if you don't mind me asking, Erica, what will you be doing, and how long will you be around?"

"First, I'll be researching the project," she told him, "doing site evaluations, making cost estimates of alternative plans, assessing market conditions and so forth. I figure I'll be spending a month or so here, and another month pulling the final report together once I get home."

"You're doing more than sniffing the wind, in other words."

She smiled. "Considerably."

"And you think you can be objective?"

She could see the man was no fool. It was not an innocent question. "I have no vested interest in this either way. The facts will speak for themselves. My job is to draw together the data and identify the issues and alternatives so that an intelligent decision can be made."

"All that, and grace us with your lovely presence."

"Thank you, but I don't know that that's relevant."

"Maybe not to Gram, but your feasibility study's not going to do me any good. So naturally, I'm looking to see what other benefits there might be," he said with a grin.

Erica glanced at Julia, who seemed busy eating, her eyes on her plate. There was a tiny smile on her lips, however. "I'm going to be awfully busy, Clay," Erica told him. "I don't think you'll see much of me."

"Now that's the first tragic thing I've heard."

This time Erica caught Julia's eye.

The woman turned to her grandson. "I think Erica

and I will be satisfied if the atmosphere is pleasant and she's able to work in peace."

"In other words, don't overdo the friendliness bit," he said.

"I think you know what I mean," Julia replied.

Clay took a couple of bites of food. "I gather, in addition to taking her into town, you probably want me to take her out to your ghost town, as well."

"That would be very nice if you would."

"It'd be a test of how much of a gentleman I am, Gram, but for you, I'll do it."

They ate for a while in silence. Erica tried to decide if Clay was as innocent as he seemed. She doubted it. Ulterior motives were likely, but did they have to do with the project, or with her?

"So, will you be staying in the guest room?" he asked.

Erica and Julia exchanged looks again.

"She'll be staying a few nights," Julia said finally, "but she hasn't firm plans beyond that."

"I told Julia I'd like to get a place in town, if I can find a short-term rental," Erica said.

"But I told her that it would be much easier if she stayed here at the ranch," Julia hastily added.

Clay didn't hesitate. "If you're asking my permission, I have no objection. Erica's welcome to stay as long as she likes."

"You're both very kind," Erica said, "but a month's a long time…"

"Which is why I thought it might be a good idea if she stayed in the little cabin. I hope I'm not out of line bringing it up," Julia said, turning to Clay, "but that way Erica would be on her own and not have a forty-mile commute each way…assuming it wasn't a problem for you, of course."

A dark look came over Clay's face. Julia seemed to notice, as well. Erica shifted uncomfortably.

"If you object to the idea, Clay, that's fine," Julia said after a short silence. "I can see it was thoughtless of me to bring it up." She gave Erica a hostess smile. "Now, if everybody's finished, I'll have Rosita bring dessert."

Clay, ignoring her, turned to Erica. "My fiancée died over ten years ago. She and I had planned to live in the little cabin, the one Gram is suggesting you use. And the only reason I hesitate is that since Laura died, well, I've left the place empty. For sentimental reasons, I guess."

"I understand, Clay," she said. "And the last thing I want is to create a problem—"

"No, let me finish." He glanced at his grandmother. "Gram's been telling me I've been clinging too hard to the past. I reckon she's right about that, but I haven't had a real good reason to change things. Now you've given me a reason."

Erica glanced at Julia, who nodded.

"Why not give it a try?" the older woman suggested. "And if it doesn't feel good to you, you can always go into town."

She could think of no other way to respond but to say, "Okay, that would be fine."

"And as for going into Red Rock, how about we leave right after lunch?"

"Great. Whatever works for you."

"That's settled then," Julia said. "I do like it when people behave with a spirit of cooperation."

"What are you saying, Gram, that I'm not a hopeless cause, after all?'' he teased, the lightness back in his voice.

"I'm saying," Julia replied with a lilt of her own, "that Erica's an even better influence than I'd hoped."

Erica wasn't sure why, but she felt herself blush. Worse, Clay noticed. She could tell by the little smile she saw at the corner of his mouth.

"Gram," he said, "are you going to ring that bell and get Rosita in here with some of that pie I've been smelling, or am I going to have to come over there and ring it myself?"

Julia picked up the bell and rang it. Then, to Erica, she said, "Don't you just love the way men always manage to make it look like they're in charge?"

Clay threw back his head and laughed. "Gram," he said, "you're not fooling a soul. You've gotten everything you want tonight, just like you always do."

"Why, Clay!"

"You know what Granddad told me once? He said, 'Son, make sure you marry a smart one, because your whole life she'll be telling you what to decide, and there's no sense spending a lifetime making stupid decisions.'"

"Hap said no such thing, you scoundrel!"

"I swear he did."

"Your grandfather and I always discussed things on an equal basis and came to joint decisions on matters that concerned us both."

Clay chuckled, giving Erica a wink.

"You're just trying to get back at me, young man. I know your tricks." Julia rang the bell again.

"Why, Gram, I'd never do that."

"Listen to this man, Erica," Julia said. "Hear that

innocent tone? I don't know how women manage to put up with men, I truly don't."

"I do," Clay replied, gazing deep into Erica's eyes. "But it's not a topic for the dinner table."

4

ERICA COULDN'T SLEEP that night. She was uncomfortable about the notion of using the cabin, but that paled by the anxiety she felt over finding herself the focus of tension between Julia and Clay. She was squarely in the middle of a family problem, and that was not a good position for an outsider. She tried to tell herself that Julia was employing her, so she shouldn't worry about what Clay thought. But it wasn't as easy to ignore the vibes between Clay and herself. The cowboy charm, his flirting with the city girl, had been just the beginning. Erica sensed he had designs on her and she wasn't so sure that was what she wanted.

Sally would have said, "What's the big deal? If he's cute and not too boring, then why not?"

Well, Clay was cute—more than cute, actually— and he hadn't bored her yet, though it was still early. Nor did she feel that he was coming on too strong. Guys had come on to her before, and she'd dealt with it. Clay could be cooled down, if he got too pushy. This problem seemed different though. She sensed a deeper need in him and it scared her— scared her because of her own vulnerability.

If a guy asked her out more than once, she made it a policy to tell him about the hepatitis. "But you won't die kissing me," she'd say puckishly. Her dates were always surprised when she told them she was ill, because it didn't show. And they'd want to know more about her disease. Her policy was to be blunt. "I could one day develop liver cancer or cirrhosis," she'd say. "There's no way of knowing what might happen." And then they'd want to know how she got it and she'd say the doctors thought from a transfusion she'd had during surgery a few years ago. Mostly guys were sympathetic, some were clearly scared by it. Quite a few wouldn't ask her out again, which was why she liked to tell them early, before any attachments were formed.

Erica wondered if she should tell Clay. Considering what had happened to his fiancée, it seemed the sooner she told him, the better. On the other hand, that might be rather presumptuous. They weren't dating, though the attraction was real enough. She decided the thing to do, probably, was wait. If things did begin to move that way, then she'd deal with it.

Having worked out that much, she managed to sleep some, but she awoke early the next morning with more feelings of anxiety. That upset her, or annoyed her, she wasn't sure which was more accurate. One thing was certain, this situation with Clay was bothering her more than it should.

Since she was awake, Erica decided to get out of bed. Dawn was just breaking and, when she peered out the window, she saw a figure moving across the lawn toward the barn. It was Clay, up early and off to work.

She watched him, noting his long strides and confident carriage. He was a man in tune with his environment, but was he in tune with his own soul? She didn't know him well enough to say, but she suspected that might be his issue.

After her shower, Erica put on jeans, a blouse and sneakers and went to the kitchen where she found Rosita shelling pecans.

"Good morning, *señorita*," the housekeeper said. "You are up early. Would you like some breakfast?"

Erica could smell the coffee and had a sudden appetite. "Sure, but you don't have to wait on me. I can pour myself some coffee, and if you point me to the toaster…"

"No, you sit down, Señorita Ross, and be comfortable. It is my job. Besides, this is my kitchen. It is easier for me, no?"

"I hate to interrupt your work."

"This can wait. What you want? Eggs? Pancakes?"

"A soft-boiled egg would be wonderful. You're sure I can't help?"

"I don't let even the *señora* cook in this kitchen, except for Christmas pudding and her special chocolate cake, which is very good. But you are very nice to say it." Rosita filled a mug with coffee and took it to her. "Cream or sugar?"

"No, thanks."

"Orange juice?"

"If it's not too much trouble."

"You are so polite, *señorita*. You must have a very wonderful mother, no?"

"I'd like to think she was wonderful, but I never knew her. She died when I was born."

Rosita frowned, a look of sorrow on her face. "Oh, so sad."

"I was raised by my father's sister, who was a very nice woman. But she and my uncle had an autistic child and they didn't have a lot of time for me." Erica wasn't quite sure why all this was tumbling out. She smiled. "But I survived."

The housekeeper had gotten a pitcher of juice from the refrigerator, poured some in a glass and put it in front of Erica. "You seem to be a nice lady, so something was good in your life."

"Life is what you make it."

"I tell that same thing to Emilio, my husband, but he says no, luck is the most important. His cousin, Juan, he won a lottery in Mexico. It was four thousand dollars, and with the money he bought a little store and now he is rich. To Emilio I say we are rich in our way, too. Rich in our mind and in our heart."

"You are very wise, Rosita."

"I am a woman, and as you must know, too, we sometimes understand these things better. The men who do, they are mostly priests."

Erica nodded. She liked Rosita. In fact, she liked everyone she'd met at the Lone Eagle. She'd have to tell Sally that people in the sticks had their redeeming qualities. She was glad for this little conversation because she was feeling better already. And the coffee was great.

"Oh, I nearly forgot to tell you, *señorita*," Rosita said. "Señor McCormick, he wants me to give you a message. He will be busy until about eleven this morning, then he will come to the house for you and show the cabin. I will have it clean so it will look pretty. The *señor*, he wants you to like it."

"You think he really does?"

"This I know, Señorita Ross. Señor McCormick,

he doesn't talk to me about the women very much, but I see some little thing happen in his eye when he speaks of you, you know what I mean?"

"What kind of thing?"

"A happy thing. And this is good, because I have not seen it for many years. Not since…well, you know about the girl he was to marry."

Erica had a sinking feeling. "Yes, I heard."

"I am not saying he thinks the same of you, but he does not have the chance for this kind of happiness and it is good to see what the pretty woman she can do to a man like Señor McCormick. He is *muy fuerte* and he needs the softness of a woman."

"Rosita, I think you misunderstand my purpose here. I'm helping Mrs. Sommers on a business project."

"Yes, I know this, but can I help it if I have the heart of a poet?"

"Poetry's fine, but that's not why I am here," Erica said.

"I am sorry, *señorita*, it is not fair to you that I say these things. I like to see people happy. Sometimes it can be a fault."

"Please, don't apologize. I just want you to understand."

"I do, very much," Rosita said. "But you must admit, Señor McCormick, he is very nice and very handsome, no?"

"Yes, I admit it," Erica said, starting to smile.

"I will say no more, then. Now is the time for you to eat."

CLAY KNEW it was a problem that Erica Ross kept popping into his mind. Whether he was counting cattle in a box canyon, administering a shot to a sick heifer, or simply staring up at the pale blue sky, he'd picture her face and feel a yearning to fill the emptiness inside him. It was that void in his gut, that awareness of need, that he noticed most. He hadn't felt that since he'd finally let go of Laura. Oh, he still felt sadness from time to time, the loss, but this feeling about his grandmother's consultant was different. This was a yearning for connection, like those empty months when he was at college and Laura was in Red Rock, dreaming dreams for them that were never to be.

Having a little extra time before he had to show Erica the cabin, Clay decided to ride up through Zuni Canyon. One of the boys had told Emilio that he'd seen an eagle's nest at the head of the canyon, and that he thought it belonged to a bald eagle. If that was true, Clay was eager to see it because there hadn't been nesting bald eagles on the ranch in his lifetime. His grandfather had seen many mating pairs in his time, but that was years ago.

As his horse plodded along the rocky trail, Clay again thought of Erica. Maybe, he told himself, his fixation wasn't due to her so much as to the emptiness in his life. Yes, that had to be it. He hardly knew Erica Ross, so it couldn't really be her. And if his thoughts dwelled on her, it was only because there'd been no one else who'd captured his imagination for so long. The good-time girls he played with were different. They were not a part of his life.

Erica, on the other hand, had sat at his dinner table. She was under his roof. And although they were at odds because she was working for Julia, she was smack-dab in the middle of his life. Which did not mean anything necessarily had to come of it. But he was intrigued and he couldn't ignore the feeling.

Maybe the surprising thing was that something like this hadn't happened sooner. People had said some cute little thing was bound to come along one day and catch his eye. But he hadn't been looking for it. On the contrary, he'd focused his energy on his work. And yet, now he found that he was torn.

Clay didn't want to make a big deal of it. Erica Ross would be leaving soon enough and that would take care of things, he reasoned. In the meantime, he was of two minds as to what to do. He either faced up to the attraction and played it out, or he made damn sure nothing came of it. Feeling the need to fight it was a pretty good indication he was afraid of what might happen, and he didn't like being afraid of anything. Besides, if he avoided her, his curiosity about her would only increase. Better, he decided, to meet the challenge head-on. That was more in keeping with his nature.

Clay finally reached the end of the canyon where the floor began rising steeply toward the rim. Emilio had told him the nest was about three-quarters of the way up the east wall. Clay gazed up at the sheer rock cliff, but couldn't spot the nest. Dismounting, he climbed up a pile of boulders, which would give him a more unobstructed view. After searching the face of the ruddy cliff for several moments, he finally spotted a tangle of black sticks on a ledge a hundred and fifty feet above him. He could barely make out three little white heads protruding from the top. The Lone Eagle was no longer alone.

It occurred to him how pleased his granddad would have been, how truly special this was, when he heard a cow bleating behind him, some distance away. Clay looked, but couldn't see anything. Climbing down from the boulders, he made his way through the brush until he came to the cow, standing next to her calf, which was stuck in a tangle of brambles. The poor little critter was sagging with exhaustion from its struggle to free itself. It had likely been caught since the day before. Clay estimated it would have been dead in a few hours if he hadn't come along.

Wading into the tangle of shrubs, he grabbed hold of the calf, which was too weak to offer much resistance. Lifting it into his arms, he carried it back to where he'd left his horse. The cow, trailing along behind, was bleating now with more urgency than before.

Throwing the feeble calf over the horse, Clay climbed into the saddle and headed for the mouth of the canyon. There were a number of cattle there and he figured the cow would tend to her calf once she was safely in the herd.

He checked his watch, noting that he would have to get back to the house if he was going to take Erica to the cabin before lunch. He needed to get cleaned up, too, since he'd be driving her into town. Julia had suggested he take her to the Cowboy Club for dinner, which struck him as a good idea. If nothing else, it would give him an opportunity to get to know her a little better. One way or another, he'd find out whether this fascination he had for her was significant or just a passing thing.

ERICA STOOD at the dining-room table, where Julia had told her to set up shop, and was studying the map of the ranch when Clay entered the room. He was cleaned up and looked terrific, just as he did the night before. Clay was a cowboy, yes, but, she was beginning to see, a cowboy of the gentlemanly variety. Why she found him so appealing, she couldn't exactly say. This was not the type of guy she normally went for. Maybe it was a subliminal thing. The rugged good looks, the *muy fuerte* quality Rosita had mentioned, could be striking a chord she wasn't previously aware of.

"Ready to have a look at that cabin?" he asked, approaching the table.

"If you are."

Coming up beside her, he glanced down at the map. She smelled that herbal cologne again. As before, it gave her a jolt.

The section of land where the movie town was located, the piece owned by Julia, was outlined in red on the map. Clay put his finger on it.

"Kind of looks like an island sitting there, doesn't it?" he said.

She knew what he was alluding to. "Access is essential, of course."

"And that's the problem."

"Would a road to it be all that disastrous?" she asked.

"A little like having to share your bathroom with your next-door neighbor," he replied.

"I haven't experienced that sort of attachment to land, but I guess I can imagine what it's like."

They both looked up from the map and into each other's eyes. There was something very strong emanating from him. It must have been the same thing

Rosita had seen happening in his eyes. It made her uneasy.

"Can you?" Clay said.

Erica glanced back down at the map. "Yes."

He let her word hang in the silence for several moments, then said, "Shall we go look at the cabin?"

"You know, Clay, I'm not so sure the cabin is such a good idea," she said, her words coming before she'd had a chance to think them through.

"Why?"

"It'd be easier if I didn't stay on the ranch."

"For who?"

"For you," she said bravely.

"I believe we've already settled this issue. No point in bringing it up again," he said, taking her arm. "Come on, let's go have a look. It might be that you won't even like the place, which would give you the excuse you need."

"I really don't need an excuse," she insisted as she went along with him.

"No, of course you don't. I shouldn't have put it that way."

Clay relaxed his grip, guiding her along now rather than taking her forcibly. She was glad because she didn't like a man thinking he could do with her as he liked. When they came to the front door, he let go of her arm entirely. Taking his hat from the chair, he opened the door, gesturing for her to go out, which she did. The sun was hot. Erica went a few steps along the walk before she stopped and turned to face him.

"Why do I feel this tension when I'm around you, Clay?" she said, letting what was on her mind spill out.

He didn't appear so much surprised by her direct-
ness as amused. He peered at her from under the
shadowed brim of his hat. The smile that followed
told her he might have misconstrued her meaning.

"*Uncomfortable* tension," she said, making sure he
got her point.

Clay shrugged. "You're a sheep in cattle country,
Erica."

She paused for a long moment before replying.
"No, I don't think that's it."

"You want me to speculate on what it might be?"

She considered the possibility. But the lilt in his
voice made her decide she might not want to hear
the answer. "No, I'm just wondering how we can
get past it."

He surprised her by putting an arm around her
shoulder and leading her toward the shiny new
pickup truck parked in the circular driveway. "As
we get better acquainted, I think the problem will re-
solve itself," he said.

Erica said nothing until they got to the truck. "I
don't want misunderstandings, Clay. I'm a serious
person. This is all business as far as I'm concerned."

"Is that another way of saying back off?"

"It's not another way of saying anything. I just
want to be clear."

He smiled. "Well, don't you worry your pretty little head about me. I may not be the smartest fella
around, but I do know that when a mustang gives
you trouble, the best solution is to change the bit."

"That must be another of your rules."

"Yes, ma'am. Cowboy Code rule number eight.
Believe me, there's a lot of wisdom in simple livin'."

He opened the door and offered his hand to help Erica climb into the cab.

She settled into the seat, feeling more emotion than she figured was warranted. She watched him come around to the driver's side and climb in beside her. He sat there for a moment, as though searching for a way to express what he was feeling.

But instead of saying anything, Clay started the engine and headed around the driveway, past the barn, corral and other outbuildings, until they were bumping along the road that led up the valley. Erica considered saying something about her illness, but the time didn't seem right.

"Do you feel as frustrated as I do?" she finally asked.

Clay nodded, saying with perfect understanding, "Yes, I guess I do."

"So what does it mean?"

There was an earnest expression on his face. "I tend to answer direct questions with direct answers."

"That's fine."

"Okay," he said. "I'm frustrated because I think it's a damn shame you're working for my grandmother."

"Why?"

"I could answer that, but I think I'll leave it to your imagination instead."

In spite of her question, Erica knew exactly what he meant. The hell of it was, she couldn't rebuke him because, in her heart of hearts, she couldn't honestly say she wasn't interested herself.

Neither of them said anything. It was as though they both knew.

Glancing over at him, she could see he was deep in thought. And the closer they got to the cabin, the more his expression changed. By the pain etched around his eyes and the tight set of his mouth, she was fairly certain that he was wrestling with demons—his loss of Laura.

They approached a thicket of cottonwoods within which Erica could make out the outline of a cabin. Clay slowed.

"My great-grandfather built this place," he said evenly, his voice low and steady. "Lived in it before he married because he didn't like the old ranch house. But it's been modernized. I think you'll find it comfortable."

Erica took a deep breath and turned to see the cabin. It was built of wood with a large stone chimney dominating one side. She climbed out of the truck. Clay joined her and they went to the door, which he opened for her.

The cabin was small, consisting essentially of two rooms, plus a kitchenette and bathroom. The furnishings were modest. The place was very clean and smelled of furniture polish and cleaning solvent, overlaid with pine air freshener. Erica slowly walked around the room, getting a sense of it. She wouldn't describe it as homey, but there was a realness about it, a solidity that came with generations of use. There was a vase of flowers on the table that Rosita must have brought from the house. A fresh stack of wood sat in the fireplace.

Erica turned to face Clay who was leaning against the door frame, one booted foot crossed over the other, his hat hanging from his hand. His expression was stoic.

"So, will you stay?" he asked simply.

Erica searched for a way to express the complexity of her feelings. Finding nothing that seemed right, she simply said, "Yes, I will."

He seemed relieved. "That's settled, then."

"A part of you must be upset," she said.

Clay reflected for a moment, then said, "Not the way you're thinking." He glanced around the room, and she could tell that a thousand memories were streaming through his mind. "I don't know if you can understand this, but when Laura and I were planning on living here, we were so young…and, well, we thought we'd have forever."

She nodded. "I do understand that, Clay. All too well."

She walked past him and out to the truck, fully realizing for the first time why she felt a connection with Clay McCormick—not just the physical attraction, but something deeper, something in his soul. He, too, had learned that "happily ever after" did not always mean forever.

5

As the highway curved around a bluff, the town of Red Rock came into view. It was a green oasis, a few square miles in size, spread leisurely over the sloping plain abutting a rust-red mountain range.

"There she is," Clay said. "If you eliminate the most obvious modern additions, it doesn't look all that different than it did a hundred years ago."

He didn't say it, but Erica was fairly certain he would have liked it better then. During most of the drive into town, Clay had chatted about Red Rock and its citizens. He'd even ventured carefully into the realm of politics, though he'd avoided topics of controversy. Erica was relieved. She was glad for the lightening of his mood.

Things had been different almost from the moment they'd left the cabin. Neither of them had said much during the drive back to the ranch house, but even so, the tension had eased. Clay, it seemed, had decided to give her a respite.

There was some kind of problem waiting for him when they'd gotten back to the ranch, so he hadn't eaten lunch with her and Julia, taking a sandwich Rosita hastily made instead, and going off to tend to business.

Julia was pleased Erica had decided to take the cabin, and noted that there was plenty of extra furniture in a storage shed, if she needed anything. Mostly they talked about the project, for which Erica was grateful. Julia hadn't felt well that morning, so lunch was the first real chance they'd had to talk today.

"I got a few things accomplished this morning while I was resting in bed," Julia had told her. "Made some calls into town. Evelyn Wilkins at the chamber of commerce is expecting you and so is Thelma Almstad at the library. They'll be good resources."

Clay had shown up a few minutes later to drive her into town, in a different mood from when she'd last seen him. All in all, by the time they entered the outskirts of Red Rock, she felt better, wondering if perhaps she'd blown things out of proportion earlier because of her own sensitivities.

"Julia told me I was to take you to the chamber of commerce," he said as he waved to the driver of a passing flatbed truck. "Anything else you want to see?"

"Nothing in particular. I'll just wander around and get the flavor of the place."

"Why don't I give you a driving tour to orient you? Between a few landmarks and the chamber map, I reckon you won't have any trouble."

"That isn't necessary, Clay. You have things to do, I know."

"It won't take but ten minutes," he said. "There's not a lot to see."

"Then I'd be grateful."

Her acceptance of his offer seemed to please him. "While we're on this side of town, I might as well show you the high school. It's just up this side street," he said, turning.

They went a block and came to a single-story brick building that had probably been built in the 1930s or 1940s. Erica estimated it would accommodate about two hundred students. She noticed the flag flying on the pole out front and a sign that said Red Rock High School and below that, Home of the Eagles. Clay stopped the truck and glanced out at the lawn, scorched in places by the summer heat.

"Did you graduate from Red Rock High?" she asked.

"Yep. Captain of the football team and class president. But that was only because I didn't have any competition to speak of. We only had one winning season while I was here and nobody wanted to be president, including me. They elected me anyway. A big fish in a very small pond."

"Was Laura the homecoming queen?"

He gave her a quirky smile tinged with sadness. "Kind of predictable, isn't it?"

"It's not surprising, Clay, let me put it that way."

"Well, everything's relative, you know. Personally, I never minded the slow pace of things around here, and the limited horizons. That was never clearer to me than when I went away to college."

"You didn't like it?"

"I saw that the outside world could be seductive and I decided I didn't want to be seduced."

"That's very insightful."

"Well, I don't claim to be stupid," he replied with a laugh, "just provincial."

She saw genuine warmth in his eyes, even a flicker of happiness. He'd ventured out of some deeper, darker place in his soul, and he seemed to be realizing it right along with her. His eyes skittered down her and he put the truck in gear.

"Why don't we swing through the nicer residential part of town, then I'll drive through the business district. The Cowboy Club's right in the middle of things. That's where we'll have dinner."

"You really don't have to entertain me, Clay, despite what Julia says."

"Oh, I'd enjoy it. In fact, seeing me come in with a pretty woman will give the boys something to talk about. Tongues'll be wagging for days."

"I'm surprised you'd consider that good."

"When you get to know me better, Erica, you'll discover I can be downright unpredictable." Then Clay did do something completely unexpected—he reached over and gave her a light pinch on the cheek, his eyes twinkling.

They drove up and down several of the finer residential streets with big two-story houses featuring attributes like cupolas, bay windows, wraparound porches and huge shade trees. Clay pointed out where the doctors, the lawyers and the bankers lived and things like how long the houses had been in the families.

After that they headed for the business district. On Main Street, Clay pulled into the Dairy Queen. Erica accepted his offer of a soft ice cream. He got each of them a small one. They sat in the truck talking and eating their cones.

"When's the last time a guy bought you an ice cream?" he asked.

"I guess in high school."

"Hasn't been quite that long for me, but almost."

"Was it Laura?" she asked.

He sighed faintly. "Yes, when her illness got so bad they told her she wouldn't be getting out of bed much anymore. Our first date was here at the Dairy Queen and she wanted our last one to be here, too. She had me drive her down so we could have one more cone together."

"Clay, that's so sad."

"Yeah, and not something to dwell on, is it?"

He changed the subject, his tone lightening the way it had before. But Erica could see how much he continued to suffer. Her heart went out to him.

After they finished eating, they drove the few blocks of the commercial district. Clay pulled over directly across the street from the Cowboy Club. He rolled down his window. "There it is."

Erica peered past him. The building was in the middle of the block, the facade made of rough-hewn boards weathered to a silvery gray. A large black-on-white sign running nearly the width of the building said Cowboy Club in bold, plain letters. There were swinging bar doors across the entrance and wooden doors set back to keep out the heat in summer and the cold in winter. It looked authentic enough.

"Cody James or Julia own most of the buildings on the block," Clay explained. "That's why you see the wooden sidewalks and the cutesy western facades. They'd like the whole town to look this way."

"Like it did a hundred years ago?"

"The Hollywood version," he replied. But he said it with a smile, not bitterly. "The chamber of commerce is over on Cottonwood Street. I'll take you there."

"Hey, Clay!" a man called from across the street.

"Well," Clay said to Erica, "speak of the devil. That's Gram's old partner, Cody James." He leaned out the window. "What's up, Cody?"

The heavyset man, wearing a huge white hat that cast a shadow over most of his corpulent body, waddled carefully to the edge of the wooden sidewalk, steadying himself with his cane. "I'm wonderin' what in tarnation you're doin' sittin' out in the sun when you could be sippin' a cool one in my establishment! Been too long since I've seen you, son."

"I'm coming by later for dinner," Clay replied. "Make sure you got a couple of buffalo steaks in the fridge."

"Ben still lives in fear of Julia comin' in the kitchen and findin' something in short supply," Cody called back, resting his hand on his huge silver belt buckle. "Don't need to worry about us runnin' out of buffalo or anything else."

"I'll count on that, Cody. See you in a few hours."

The man saluted him and shuffled toward the entrance to the club.

"Poor old Cody," Clay said, looking after him. "Had a stroke last year and he's been pretty frail ever since."

"Yet he still works?"

"If you want to call it that. Dax Charboneau runs the club to all intents and purposes. Cody doesn't have anything else in his life, so he devotes himself to his business interests as best he can."

"Doesn't he have a family?"

"Never married. The only relative he talks about is a niece in New York City, of all places. People wonder what's going to happen to his interest in the club once he passes away. Could be it's going to end up in her hands."

Erica wondered if Clay dreaded the prospect of half of the Cowboy Club being owned by a New Yorker. "How do you feel about that?" she asked.

"Not rightly any of my business. But I do feel sorry for the old codger."

"Why? Because he doesn't have any immediate family to leave his money to?"

Clay shrugged. "Could be."

Erica knew she had no business taking the conversation in this direction, but she said it anyway. "What are your plans for the Lone Eagle once you're gone?"

He rubbed his jaw. "I guess I always assumed I'd have children to pass it on to. But I guess there won't be any—unless I do something about it, huh?"

"It does take some effort," she said, arching an eyebrow, "if not intention."

Clay rolled up the window so the air-conditioning wouldn't be wasted. "You've got a point, Erica." He pulled back into the street. As they rode along, he said, "So, do you have family?"

She told him about growing up in her aunt and uncle's home, without going into detail.

"Why didn't you stay with your father after your mother died?"

"Dad was an air force officer and didn't think the military was the best environment for a kid without a mother," she told him. "It would have been hard for him as a single parent to try and raise me, which was why he sent me to live with his sister. He did remarry before he retired, though. His wife is a Filipina and already had a couple of kids when they married. There was some talk briefly about bringing me to live with them, but Dad figured I was better off where I was. I seldom saw him after he married. I think I went to their home twice, though he's come to see me three or four times."

"Where does he live?"

"In L.A. He runs a swimming-pool maintenance business. The last time I saw him was two years ago when I flew to California for the wedding of my stepbrother, Randall."

"How was it?"

"Nobody was unfriendly, but I felt like a distant relative. My father did dance with me at the wedding reception. I don't know if he realized it, but it's the only time he's ever held me in his arms...at least since I was a little kid."

Clay glanced over at her, apparently having heard the quaver in her voice. Her eyes shimmered, embarrassing her. She didn't know why she'd gotten so emotional, or why she'd told Clay these things.

He pulled up in front of a small storefront building with stenciled lettering in the window reading Chamber of Commerce, Red Rock, Colorado. He put his arm on the back of the seat so that his hand rested behind her.

"I'm sorry, Erica."

"Sorry?" she said, looking at him inquisitively.

"Sorry that happened to you."

"Oh." She assumed the placid expression she normally did when talking about her family. "Well, it's ancient history."

"Sure, but things like that can affect you for a long time. A real long time. Sometimes forever."

She knew he was speaking from experience—

about the ten years since Laura had died—and his pain made her feel a certain kinship with him again. Still, she didn't want to be maudlin. It wouldn't do either of them any good to dwell on the past. "Yes, I know you're right, Clay. But I refuse to let my father have control over my happiness. It's my life."

He nodded. "You're right. Gram is always saying that to cry over a troubled past is a waste of good tears."

"Is that in the Cowboy Code?"

"Honorary."

They regarded each other, her eyes still glistening. Oddly, she felt he understood exactly what she was feeling. Maybe that's why it didn't surprise her when he reached over and took her hand. The gesture felt warm and natural. And it sent a twinge through her.

"Come on," he said, giving her fingers a quick squeeze before letting go. "I'll take you inside and introduce you to Evelyn."

Clay got out of the truck and met her on the sidewalk. They went inside where they were greeted by a plump middle-aged woman with a mop of red curls. She took the half-frame reading glasses off her nose, allowing them to hang from her neck.

"Why, Clay McCormick," she said. "You're the very last person I'd ever expect to come walking into the chamber office. Don't tell me you've bought a business and are joining up."

He laughed. "I've gotten a bit too much sun a time or two, but not so often I've lost my mind. No, Evelyn, I brought by a business associate of Julia's to meet you."

The woman turned to Erica. "Oh, yes, Miss Ross,

isn't it? Julia told me you were on the way in this afternoon—I wouldn't have thought with Clay's help, however." She looked her over none too discreetly. "On the other hand, maybe I shouldn't be surprised. Clay, I think I've just discovered your Achilles' heel!"

He chuckled, dismissing the comment, though he did blush. "I can see it's time to skedaddle." He went to the door where he stopped with his hand on the knob. "Erica, if we meet at the Cowboy Club at seven, will that give you enough time?"

She checked her watch. "That should work."

"This is the late night at the library, isn't it, Evelyn?"

"Yes, Clay, it is."

"You'll give Erica a map and show her how to get there?"

"Certainly."

"I'll be seeing to my business, then," he said. "See you later, Erica. Evelyn."

"Bye, Clay." She watched him return to his truck, swing up into the driver's seat and head on up the street. Then she turned her attention to Erica, who'd also been looking after him.

"Isn't he just scrumptious?" Evelyn said.

"Clay's a nice guy."

"Oh, that's not the half of it. If I were twenty years younger, that man would either have to marry me or shoot me!" She giggled. "But I'm not, so I guess I'll have to stick to chamber business. Come," she said, turning from the window, "let me show you the packet I've gotten together for you."

Erica went with the woman, but her mind was still on Clay McCormick. The feel of his hand when he'd taken hers was fresh in her mind. And her heart was still beating nicely. She knew exactly what was happening. Despite herself, she was getting a crush on the guy, the kind of crush a teenage girl would get on the captain of the football team.

ERICA LEFT the library around six-thirty. She'd found some good historical material on Red Rock, including a short book on the Hollywood connection that had been written in the sixties. The most useful information was in the packet Evelyn Wilkins had gathered for her. The piece she'd found most fascinating was a booklet about the history of Red Rock, especially the section on the Cowboy Club. In the 1890s there had actually been a gunfight in the place between the local sheriff, Buck Talbot, and a highwayman on the run from the Oklahoma Territory, a fellow named Hank Thomas. After all the shooting was over, Talbot had taken a bullet in the leg and Thomas had been shot in the chest. The sheriff recovered, but Thomas died three days later.

Erica also found an account of the Indian raids Clay had told her about and other fascinating stories and anecdotes. Julia's theme park would not have to rely on fantasy, there was plenty of local legend to draw from. It was also interesting that some of the material had been used by the scriptwriters for several of the films that had been shot in Red Rock.

As she made her way to the Cowboy Club, Erica got more nervous. She really had mixed feelings about Clay. On the one hand, she had this crush; on the other, she knew it was perfectly ridiculous to even think that way. When she reached Main Street, she could see the Cowboy Club in the middle of the block. It was still quarter till the hour, so she decided to go in the drugstore on the corner. There were a few items she wanted to pick up.

After she made her purchases, she got an idea. "Is there a pay phone nearby?" she asked the tottery old proprietor, a skinny little man with huge hearing aids.

"There's one in back you can use, miss," he said. "In that corner behind the cosmetics."

Erica went to the phone and, using her calling card, rang Sally Nobel in Denver. Sally had just gotten home from work.

"So, how's it going?" Sally chirped.

"Sort of like a crazy movie." Erica recounted the first couple days of her visit, mentioning Clay several times.

"I think he sounds wonderful!"

"Not wonderful, Sally, unique, different."

"But you said he was good-looking."

"*Very* good-looking. I've got a thing for him, I admit it. But he's a cowboy. One with a big ranch, admittedly, but this is his life, and I do mean his *life*, Sally."

"So what? Or are you complaining because he isn't marriage material?"

"Lord, that's the furthest thing from my mind. Let's say it upsets me that I'm attracted to him."

"Why?"

"Well, because…"

"Yeah?"

Erica sighed. "He's vulnerable."

"What does that mean? That he's got a crush on you, too?"

"Maybe."

"I don't think he's going to dissolve into tears if your interests are limited to having a little fun," Sally said. "Don't forget, men are born for fun without obligation. Think one will complain when that's all you want? I don't think so."

"I'm not so sure I want that, Sally. In fact, I'm fairly certain it would be a bad idea. It could only lead to problems."

"What kind of problems? Professional? Personal? His? Yours?"

Erica hesitated. "All of the above."

"You know what I think?" Sally said after several moments of reflection. "I think you've really, truly, seriously got a thing for this guy."

"No more than he's got for me."

"What are you most afraid of? Hurting him or being hurt?"

"Oh, Sally, I don't know. Both."

"Are you sure that's where things are? I mean, how long have you known the guy? Two days? Maybe you're imagining things."

"No," Erica said. "I can feel it. Every time I look into his eyes, I get shivers. It scares me a little, to tell you the truth. This is not me, Sally. This is weird, like some sort of out-of-body experience."

"Has he kissed you?"

"No, of course not!"

"Oh, sorry."

"You see," Erica said. "The whole thing is stupid. I don't even understand my own feelings."

"Hmm. Well, I've got a little advice for you."

"What?"

"Relax."

"Huh?"

"I said relax. Don't be so damn uptight. Honestly, Erica, sometimes you're your own worst enemy."

"Hey, whose side are you on?"

"Listen, kiddo, why don't you give yourself permission to have a little fling with your cowboy and stop worrying about it? That's the way to handle this. Trust me. I know you, I know what you need. Go have a nice dinner and forget about everything but the dimple in his chin."

"Clay doesn't have a dimple in his chin."

"I think you know what I mean."

"It's his eyes, Sally," Erica said. "They're the most incredible color. Like a wolf. A very nice wolf."

"Oh, boy, you do have a crush on the guy."

"And it'll end in disaster, I know it will."

There was a long silence.

"Sally?"

"I don't think you heard a word I said."

"Yeah, you said relax and have fun. But it's hard, considering."

"You can do it for one night, can't you? Just give yourself permission to let loose. Then tomorrow you can reassess everything."

"Okay," Erica said. "That sounds like a good plan. I can do that. I mean, that's what I've been doing ever since Tom and I broke up."

"There you go."

"Listen, Sally, thanks so much for propping me up. This isn't at all like me. I mean, when was the last time I got screwy over a guy? I was hurt when Tom broke our engagement, but I understood. I wasn't confused. Not like I am now."

"That's what friends are for. Now go have some fun with your cowboy."

"I'll do my best." She hung up the phone, feeling much better. Now all she had to do was go meet Clay. And have a good time.

6

AS SHE SIPPED her cola at the bar, Erica studied the colorful interior of the Cowboy Club, knowing she'd never seen anything even remotely like it in her life. The club was much larger than it had appeared to be from the outside. Walking into the place, the first thing she'd noticed in the main room was the long mahogany bar that looked as if it might have been hauled out West a hundred years earlier. There was a long narrow mirror in an old gilt frame on the wall behind the bar, and an enormous buffalo head hung over it. There were also a couple of deer, elk and an assortment of horns and antlers, antique guns, a huge buffalo rifle and various Native-American artifacts. On other walls there were old oil paintings of western scenes, mostly involving cowboys, Indians and animals.

Across from the bar and in the adjoining dining room there were dozens of tables topped with blue-and-white-gingham tablecloths. A number of wagon-wheel and lantern chandeliers hung from the ceiling. Each table had a drippy candle and most were occupied by townsfolk—men in western attire or work clothes, women in cotton dresses or jeans. A lively buzz filled the air.

At the back of the club was a small dance floor and bandstand. She pictured Julia there, under a spotlight singing to a hushed crowd. The sign at the door said Live Music and Dancing Tonight, but there were no musicians present and the floor was empty. It was still early, though.

Erica had seen no sign of Clay, and she hadn't noticed his truck out front, but it was only a few minutes after seven, so it was too early to worry. No one had spoken to her other than the bartender, an affable man with a large handlebar mustache. Still, quite a few people had looked her over, including the men lined up at the bar. Erica figured the fact that she was a stranger must have been the reason, though she suspected the snug fit of her jeans might have been a factor, as well.

There was an outburst of laughter at the far end of the bar where Cody James was holding court, surrounded by three or four cronies. Cody had a florid face and the air of a proprietor, though from what she'd heard, Dax Charboneau really ran the place. Still, Cody was interesting to watch.

In truth, everything about the place was interesting. Erica hadn't been able to put her finger on what it was, exactly, that struck her. The Cowboy Club had a sort of out-of-this-world feel to it—not like a movie set, because everything was obviously completely authentic. Still, the place seemed larger than life somehow. And that intrigued her.

"Excuse me, honey," came a woman's voice behind her. "Has anybody offered you a menu?"

Erica turned on her bar stool to face a smiling round-faced woman of fifty or so with an enormous cloud of white hair and coal-black, inch-long eyelashes. She wore a lacy, white peasant blouse that rested off her plump shoulders and a loose Mexican skirt. Erica figured it must be Wanda Ramirez, the hostess Julia had told her about.

"No, not yet."

"I must have been in back when you came in," she said, handing Erica a menu. "If you'd like me to put your name on the waiting list for a table, let me know."

"I'm meeting someone and I believe we've already got a reservation."

"Who are you having dinner with, if you don't mind me asking?"

"Clay McCormick."

The woman's eyebrows rose. "You must be the consultant working for Julia Sommers."

"Yes," Erica said. "Erica Ross."

"I'm Wanda Ramirez," the woman replied, offering her hand. "I've heard about you."

"Word sure does travel fast."

"Small town."

"Wanda!" came a voice from the entrance. "What does it take to get a table in this joint?"

The hostess looked over her shoulder. "Hold your horses, Cyrus. I'll be there in a minute." She rolled her eyes. "Believe it or not, this is a swank place," she said to Erica. "It's some of our customers that have no class. Excuse me, will you?" She went off, swishing her skirt. Greeting the man at the door, she led him into the dining room without breaking stride.

No sooner had they disappeared than a couple of cowboys entered the club. The new arrivals were both young, the taller one resembling Clay a little, except that he was thinner and had a drooping mustache.

Erica turned her attention to the menu. There was a variety of western and southwestern dishes, with many featuring buffalo—ribs, filets, rib eye, skirt steak and more. There was also quite a bit of beef, some chicken, trout and Mexican dishes. The special appeared to be a dish called cowboy stew, which included beef, shrimp, buffalo, vegetables, mushrooms and buttermilk mashed potatoes. Though her taste tended to run to lighter fare, Erica had to admit the menu sparked her appetite.

Checking her watch again, she set the menu on the bar and picked up her cola, wondering if Clay had gotten held up with business. That had to be it because he surely wouldn't stand her up—at least she hoped not, considering she'd gotten herself into a real positive frame of mind and was looking forward to the evening.

Peering toward the end of the bar, Erica made eye contact with Cody James. He knocked back a shot of bourbon and called over the bartender. They exchanged a brief word or two and the bartender made his way to her end of the bar.

"Excuse me, ma'am, but would you be Miss Ross by any chance?"

"Yes, I'm Erica Ross."

"Well, Mr. James, one of the owners, was wondering if you'd care to join him for a drink."

She glanced at Cody, whose red bulbous nose was evident even at a distance. He grinned and nodded. Erica knew that in a small town, the more people you established friendly relations with, the better off you were, especially when you might be needing information or advice.

"I don't care for a drink," she said, finishing the

last of her cola, "but I'd like very much to meet Mr. James."

Getting up from the bar stool, Erica made her way down the bar, causing heads to turn as she went. By the time she reached Cody James, he was beaming.

"Evenin', Miss Ross," he said, offering his hand. "Excuse me for not gettin' up, but I'm a little gimpy these days."

"I understand," she said, taking his hand. "Perhaps I should have come to introduce myself sooner. Mrs. Sommers said I should be sure and say hello."

"She's a sweetheart, Julia is. I've loved that woman for years, which tells you a lot about her, considerin' we were partners, which is almost as stressful as bein' married." He glanced toward the entrance. "Didn't I see you with Clay earlier?"

"Yes, we were set to meet here at seven. He should be arriving at any time."

"That's what I thought." Cody glanced at the clock. "He's a mite late, ain't he?"

"I'm sure he'll be along."

"I can't rightly apologize for him when I'm keepin' you standin' myself. Charlie," he said to the man next to him, "would you mind slidin' down some so the young lady can sit here and chat with me?"

The man moved off the stool and Cody patted the seat with his pudgy hand.

"Sit yourself down here, little lady."

Erica climbed up on the stool as the men politely turned away to other conversations. Cody gave her a warm, but slightly bleary-eyed smile.

"I hear tell you'll be helpin' Julia with her ghost-town theme park."

"I'm doing a feasibility study, yes."

"Well, it ain't rightly any of my business, but I'm not shy about expressin' my opinions. Personally, I think for that project to succeed, it's got to be closely tied to Red Rock. The services and attractions in town will determine whether or not Julia can make a go of it. The place can't stand on its own, in my view."

"You make a good point, Mr. James."

"I keep tellin' Julia she runs a risk by locatin' it clear out on the Lone Eagle. She'd be better off to move everything to a site closer to town."

"I'll be looking at that," Erica said noncommittally.

"It won't surprise you that I have a couple of plots in mind, both of which I happen to own."

Erica smiled. "No, that wouldn't surprise me at all, Mr. James."

"Please, we can hardly do business friendly-like if you call me Mr. James. It's Cody."

She nodded.

Cody James glanced over at the bartender. "Richie, this young gal needs another drink. What you havin', honey?"

"I had a cola, but I think I'd like mineral water this time," she replied.

"Bring the girl some bubble water," Cody said, turning his attention back to her. "I don't mean to stick my nose where it don't belong, but I reckon you're hearin' a lot of contradictory stories about which way the wind is blowin'. Just so you don't think Julia is a little old lady with a crazy dream, you ought to know eighty to ninety percent of the town is behind her. The resistance comes from some ranchers who oppose any development whatsoever, people like her own grandson."

"I'm very much aware of that," she replied.

"I expect Julia's filled you in, but it don't hurt none to hear it from several people. And it's no generational thing, either," Cody added. "Julia and I are gettin' on in years, but my partner, Dax Charboneau, is a young buck, same as Clay. You might do well to talk to him. I'm sorry Dax ain't here now or I'd introduce you. He's down in New Orleans, takin' care of some personal business. That's where he's from, you know. New Orleans."

"I've heard about Mr. Charboneau, as well."

When the barkeep brought Erica her water, Cody pointed to his empty shot glass, which was promptly filled with bourbon. The old fellow drank it half down, then carefully set the glass back on the bar.

"Would I be out of line to ask what your initial feelins are about the project?"

He *was* out of line, but Erica wasn't going to tell him that. "It's much too early for me to draw even preliminary conclusions. I haven't even see the site yet."

Cody scratched his head. "When you do have a look, keep in mind how far it'll be from Red Rock."

Erica was beginning to get a funny feeling. An idea struck her. "Cody, you haven't discussed that particular aspect—the possibility of choosing a site closer to town—with Clay, have you?"

A wary frown creased his forehead. "He didn't tell you that, did he?"

Erica shook her head.

Cody gave a weary sigh. "But I just confirmed your suspicions, right?"

She nodded.

He raised a cautioning finger. "I'm a friend of Julia's and loyal to her, but business does sometimes make for strange bedfellows. I'd appreciate it if you didn't make it look quite as conspiratorial as it seems, should you decide to mention this to anyone."

"Like Julia, for example?"

"Like Julia," Cody said, finishing off his bourbon.

Erica took a long drink of mineral water.

"Julia used to tell me I should never drink and discuss business," Cody said. "I reckon time has proved her right. For the record, I want to emphasize Clay and me ain't had any formal discussions. It's mostly been idle conversation."

"I'm a consultant," Erica told him with a smile, "not a gossip."

"You seem as bright as you are pretty," he replied, giving her a wink. Cody fingered his empty shot glass as he peered around the room. "Well, speak of the devil. Look who just walked in."

She turned to see Clay McCormick at the door, chatting with Wanda. Erica imagined that he'd asked about her and the hostess was pointing her out. Cody, meanwhile, was waving for Clay to join them.

When Erica saw him coming their way, her heart gave a little lift, and she felt the warmth of expectation. He sauntered down the bar, slapping hands with a couple of other patrons, obviously in an upbeat mood.

"Evenin', everybody!" he said, reaching them. He

directed a cordial grin especially at her. "Sorry to be late, Erica."

"No problem," she said.

Their eyes locked, unspoken messages passing between them. She was the one to look away first.

"Cody and I have been getting acquainted," she said.

"And I said a little too much," Cody said bluntly. "Told her about that piece of land I've got out on the west side of town."

Clay looked back and forth between them. He seemed to sense what had transpired. "So Erica obviously knows we've discussed the possibilities for it."

"And I assured her that's all we've done—just talked about it."

"The disadvantages of small-town life can be as significant as the advantages," Clay said to her, as though explaining. "But then, I reckon most folks tend to look out for themselves first and foremost, no matter where they live."

"As Cody says, business sometimes makes for strange bedfellows," she replied.

"I have a feeling it's time for us to have dinner," Clay said. "Wanda tells me our table is ready."

Erica was glad. She got to her feet, offering her hand to Cody. "It was a pleasure meeting you," she said.

"The pleasure was all mine," he replied a bit sheepishly. "Enjoy your dinner now, you two. Let me know if they don't treat you right."

Clay took Erica's arm. "See you later, Cody."

He led her toward the dining room, where Wanda Ramirez was waiting. As she walked alongside

Clay, Erica watched him exchange greetings with other diners. Even though the place was filled with cowboys, ranchers, businesspeople and community leaders, it was apparent that Clay was well liked and had stature in the community. Wanda took them to a corner booth large enough to seat six, though it was set for two. It had probably been specially requested.

"So," he said as they settled into the booth, "regular little sleuth, aren't you?"

His tone indicated amusement, so she didn't take offense, though she did wonder what he was really thinking—and implying. "I listen to what people tell me," she said. "I don't know if that makes me a sleuth."

"Cody's friendship is important to Julia," Clay said, his tone growing more serious. "I'd appreciate it if you didn't let her think he'd betrayed her."

"Was it a betrayal?"

"No. Sometime ago I realized my best shot at keeping that theme park off my ranch was to arrange for it to be located elsewhere," he said. "One day, Cody, who'd been thinking along the same lines, came to me with the idea of putting the park on his land. He knew how I felt and figured I'd be an ally. That doesn't make him a bad guy. He's a businessman, looking to make a buck. I suggested he talk to Julia about his site, but told him to leave me out of it, which he agreed was important if he didn't want to get scalped. What I'm saying is, it would be a lot easier for everybody if Julia was sort of left in the dark as to how it came about."

"You're asking me to withhold information from my employer," she said.

"All I ask is that if you have to say something, make it look like the initiative came from me."

"But you just said it came from Cody, didn't you?"

"Rule ten of the Cowboy Code, Erica. 'If you mean to kill some SOB on horseback, don't shoot at the horse.'"

"Meaning?"

"Julia's going to do what she's going to do, regardless. So, it seems to me there's no point in upsetting a lifelong friendship if you don't have to."

"For that, you're willing to take the blame?"

"I'm a blood relation, Erica. Gram wouldn't think twice about thrashing me, but she won't stop loving me, no matter what. Not true of Cody. Besides which, he's old and not in good health. They wouldn't have much time to make peace."

"You really think Julia would be that upset?"

"The theme park's become a deeply personal issue, not just a business matter. There's emotion on all sides. Why cause needless unhappiness?"

Clay's attitude impressed her. It was loving, and it was self-sacrificing to be willing to take the blame. She wondered if it was genuine, or if he had some other motive she couldn't see.

"A normal part of my study would involve looking at alternative sites," she said. "I guess there's no reason to tell Julia that people are conspiring to get her to move the project to a location closer to town, not if lifelong friendships are at stake."

"Thanks, Erica."

"But it won't influence my analysis, Clay," she warned him. "You might as well know that going in."

"Sweetheart, I wasn't acquainted with you five minutes before I could tell you're a woman of integrity. The last thing I'd do would be to try to influence your study of the project."

"Is that true, Clay?"

He peered at her with those wolflike eyes. "Absolutely." Then, reaching across the table, he put his hand on hers. "You might as well know the truth. I care more about you than whatever it is you're going to put in that report."

Erica gazed at his large, warm hand. She felt the electricity pass from his fingers to hers, and a pang of longing coursed through her. Her first thought was to squelch the feeling, to tell herself that it was the Cowboy Club, the atmosphere, the mood she was in—anything but that she found Clay McCormick special.

But why was that? It wasn't a lifetime commitment, after all, but a flirtation, the equivalent of a vacation romance. No strings, no promises. Even Sally had prodded her, given her the go-ahead.

But now that she was with Clay, sitting in the Cowboy Club, a thousand different emotions flooded her. Her emotions were heightened, everything seemed larger than life, bigger, different.

Erica thought of the things Julia had told her about the club—that the place was romantic with a capital _R_, harkening back to a different time when men and women seemed to be larger than life. But being with Clay now, Erica knew it wasn't only that. It had something to do with that moment back at the little cabin, when Clay had talked about "forever," and how his and Laura's love had been cut short when she died.

There was a soul-deep connection between them that couldn't be denied. One based on the pain they had each experienced. The question was, what did that mean? And more important still, what did she want it to mean?

7

JOHN AND KATE MACINNES, Clay's best friends in Red Rock, came to the table as he and Erica were finishing their mud pie and buffalo chips, which is what they called the huge chocolate-chip cookies they served at the Cowboy Club. After introducing his friends to Erica, Clay invited the MacInneses to join them for coffee while they listened to the Pritchard Boys Band playing their first set.

John, a rancher, had graduated from Red Rock High two years ahead of Clay. He was tall and sinewy, more ruggedly good-looking than handsome. Kate, just a year older than Clay, had a terrific figure and the most beautiful golden-blond hair Clay had ever seen. When he was a freshman, he'd had a big crush on her. But even as a sixteen-year-old sophomore, Kate was already in love with John MacInnes, the state junior-rodeo champion and one of the biggest heartthrobs in western Colorado. For a couple of years John toured on the professional-rodeo circuit, but then he broke his back riding bulls and retired to ranching.

The band was on their break and it was quiet enough to talk. Kate immediately engaged Erica in conversation, and Clay and John naturally began to discuss the cattle business. John described a new breed of longhorn he'd introduced to his herd, but

Clay was only half listening. He could hardly take his eyes off Erica and couldn't stop himself from eavesdropping on her and Kate. It was odd, but seeing the two of them talking gave him a funny feeling. Kate had been Laura's first cousin and the four of them had double-dated some. Erica seemed perfectly comfortable with Kate. They were both extremely attractive women and nice, nice people. Laura had been like that, too, and he couldn't help drawing comparisons.

Once John had finished his story about the longhorns, Kate managed to include them in the women's conversation. "Clay," she said, "I can't tell you how good it is to see you out and having fun. You were in that shell of yours much too long."

"I just needed something worth coming out for," he said, giving Erica a wink.

"Don't believe a word of it," Erica said to the others. "His grandmother made him bring me here so I could see the club. He's doing his duty."

"If Clay McCormick does his duty," John said, "he does it *his* way or he doesn't do it at all."

"John, you old cowpuncher," Clay said, "don't tell the lady all my secrets. You're crimpin' my style."

"Just be careful, Erica, if he gets you on the dance floor," John said. "He and Laura won the Red Rock dance contest two years runnin'. They were fabulous."

The mention of Laura put an uneasy pall over the conversation, which John didn't realize until too late. He shifted uncomfortably and took a hasty slug of coffee.

"Clay is a great dancer," Kate said, smoothing things. "I can attest to that myself."

"*Was*, Katie," Clay said. "*Was*."

"Well, the band's coming back for another set," she noted. "Maybe you can limber up those old arthritic joints and find out if you've still got it. I'm sure Erica will forgive you stumbling a bit. Meanwhile I'm going to take Mr. Foot-in-Mouth and give him a workout. Come on, John, let's go."

The two of them went off as the band began its next set. Clay and Erica looked after them.

"They are such nice people," Erica said.

"Yeah, I love them both."

"I gathered it was mutual, but Kate did complain that they hardly ever see you."

"John and I have a beer now and again, but being a bachelor, it's a little hard socializing with a married couple. Can't exactly have them over to dinner."

"I don't know that you couldn't, especially if you had a date."

"I don't date, Erica."

"Oh?"

"Let's say I just haven't made time for it."

"I see."

She stared down at her hands, seemingly aware of the awkwardness he felt. He took in the warm glow of her skin in the candlelight. It made him want to touch her face, kiss her lips.

"Or, it could be I just haven't met anybody worth the trouble," he said.

"Relationships do take time and energy."

He hesitated, then said, "Can I be blunt?"

She lifted her eyes, pushing her soft brown hair

back over her ear. There was both anticipation and uncertainty in her expression.

"I'd like to make an exception with you," he told her.

She searched his eyes for meaning, then reflected. "Well, this sort of is a date, isn't it?"

"I'd like to remove the 'sort of' part from the equation."

"What, exactly, are you saying, Clay?"

"That I brought you here for me, not Julia. And I'd like to think you came because you wanted to spend time with me, get to know me better. Not because of the project."

"You can be very direct, can't you?"

"I'd like you to dance with *me*, the ranch hand you thought you were picking up on the highway, not Julia Sommers's grandson."

"Okay," she said. "I'd like to dance with you. And I'll try to forget who you are."

He liked that she could look him in the eye and say that. Dancing wasn't really the point, and Erica knew that as well as he. What mattered was that he had asked her to put aside her business obligations—to respond to him as a man, open herself to possibilities. And she was saying that she would.

They slid out of the booth and he put his hand on her waist as they made their way to the dance floor. The band was playing a ballad. The floor was small, but there were only half a dozen couples on it. Clay gathered her close and Erica melted right into his arms. She fit perfectly and felt as soft and supple as she smelled sweet. He inhaled the scent of her hair and was overwhelmed by a desire he hadn't felt in years. Not since Laura.

THEY DANCED the rest of the set. They did the two-step, they waltzed, they danced to rock and roll and to ballads. And to her surprise, Erica never once felt like a stranger in his arms, perhaps because their bodies worked so well together, almost with the familiarity of lovers. Kate MacInnes was right—Clay was a very good dancer.

John and Kate had danced most of the set as well, but were already waiting at the table when Erica and Clay got back.

"Clay, looks like it didn't take you long to get the rust off," Kate said.

"My partner is inspiring," he said.

"I bet he secretly practices in his room all the time," Erica said.

Clay had slid into the booth next to her and had an arm behind her, resting it on the back of the banquette. He played with the ends of her hair as he spoke, and she could feel the electricity between them.

"Dancing is all chemistry," he said. "You and your partner either have it, or you don't."

"My, Erica," Kate said. "I think you just got a very big compliment."

She was a little embarrassed, but in spite of that, being with Clay was starting to feel natural, and, in an unexpected way, safe. And she liked his friends. She also liked—for one night at least—being able to forget everything and have some fun. That's what Sally had advised.

"Listen," John said, "I've got a great idea. How about we get us a couple of six-packs and drive up to Flat Iron Rock? Wouldn't that be a hoot?"

"John," Kate said, "don't you think we're beyond that? Or are you trying to relive your youth?"

"That's the point, honey. I'm saying let's take a walk down memory lane. How long since any of us have been up there? Ten years? And it's a beautiful night. Erica won't get a better view of Red Rock."

"What's Flat Iron Rock?" she asked.

"The parking spot west of town where all the kids go to neck," Clay explained.

She felt herself flush. "That's what I suspected."

"The view *is* lovely," Kate said.

"And it's a beautiful night," John added. "I remember having some great times up there."

Kate gave her husband a jab with her elbow. "Cad."

"They were all with you, honey. No need to get bent out of shape."

"That's not the point, John MacInnes!"

He scratched his head. "Well, what *is* the point?"

"Oh, God," Kate said, rolling her eyes.

Everybody laughed.

"I don't remember you ever complaining when I took you up there to smooch, Katie," he said. "In fact, often as not, it was your idea!"

Kate jokingly gave Erica a look of utter disgust. "My husband's cute, but he's got the social graces of a rodeo clown." She looked back and forth between Erica and Clay. "You two interested in a drive in the moonlight? It'll be one way to shut him up."

Erica glanced at Clay and shrugged. "It's up to you."

"The view *is* nice."

"Let's do it then," Kate said. "John and I'll pick up the beer and we'll meet you there."

"Yahoo!" John exclaimed as they slid out of the booth. "Let's go."

Erica and Clay exchanged amused looks. He again put his hand on hers. "Sure you don't mind?"

"Julia assured me you're a gentleman."

"She's never been with me to Flat Iron Rock," he replied.

Clay put some bills on the table and they made their way out of the Cowboy Club. The place was really jumping now with the large crowd and loud music. Erica could see why Julia loved it so. If she lived in Red Rock, she'd be spending a lot of time at the Cowboy Club, too.

By the time they'd threaded through the throng and got outside, John and Kate had already disappeared. Clay was parked in the next block. As they strolled in the soft evening air, Erica slipped her arm in his.

"It is a lovely evening," she said.

Clay took a deep breath. "And you won't find air like this in Denver."

"You're right about that."

They passed a middle-aged couple and Clay exchanged a greeting with them. After a few more steps he said, "So, are you a city girl? Deep in your heart?"

"It's all I've ever known, Clay. I've driven through small towns, but that's about it."

He patted the hand resting on his arm, a sly grin on his face. "Maybe I should ask you again *after* you've been to Flat Iron Rock."

She stopped and turned to him, suddenly wanting to see his face. The lights from the club and the streetlight were faint, but good enough to see his eyes. There was a glint in them that promised fun, excitement, temptation. And she wasn't completely sure how she felt about that. "What are you trying to do, Clay? Seduce me, or scare me?"

"Neither. Reassure you, that's all."

She laughed, pleased that he was able to break the tension. "Yeah, sure. I bet you were the scourge of Flat Iron Rock when you were a kid. The girls probably lined up for a ride up there with Clay McCormick."

He gave her a look of mock horror. "Do I really strike you as that type?"

"Well, you are an awfully good dancer."

"Yeah, but a dancer with a heart of gold."

She laughed again. Throwing her head back, she looked up at the stars. There seemed to be a million of them. She tilted her head, momentarily resting it on his shoulder, and drew in a long calming breath.

As she heard the steady thump of Clay's heart, she felt his arm snake across her waist, drawing her body flush against him. Her back was pressed to his torso and waist, her leg was against his. And though he was much taller, it felt natural to be so close to him. What she wasn't sure of was why that was so.

But she didn't have time to think about it because Clay lowered his head. She felt his warm breath on her cheek, and then he turned her into his arms and gently kissed her. For a moment she almost forgot to breathe. She relaxed then, long enough to fall into the kiss, to let the world around her slip away. And when she finally pulled away from him and looked into those wolflike gray eyes again, she saw that he, too, had been affected by the kiss.

"That was nice," he murmured. "Very nice."

When she didn't say anything he traced her lower lip with his index finger. "Are you having a good time?"

"Yes." Even to herself, her voice sounded tentative, wistful. "And you?"

"Best time ever." He gave a reflective sigh. "It's been a long time, Erica. So, it's practically like a new thing."

Neither of them spoke again as they came to his pickup. Clay opened the door and helped her climb in. As he made his way around to the driver's side, Erica thought about how good she felt. There was something elemental about this, something innocent and exhilarating. She couldn't recall feeling this way with Tom or any of the other men she'd known. Oh, sure, she'd known excitement, and even love, but this was like being sixteen again. And though she knew there were dangers in that, she didn't want to think about them right now.

Clay started the engine and turned on the radio, tuning in a soft country-and-western ballad. Erica wasn't a big fan of that kind of music, but she did listen to it occasionally. He gave her a warm smile and pulled into the street.

"I've got a confession to make," he said, shifting the gears.

"What's that?"

"The reason I was late tonight is because I got waylaid by Alma Jones."

"Who's that?"

"One of Red Rock's more colorful characters. She came here from Montana, oh, about fifty years ago. She's a Native American and she married Arley Jones, one of the local boys, before World War II.

Anyway, Arley died a few years back, leaving Alma the feed store. Long and short of it is, Alma claims she has a sort of second sight.

"So I was there, in the feed store, minding my own business, settling up with Bob Smitts, the clerk, when Alma comes up and grabs my hand, insisting she had to tell me something...something real important."

Erica turned to him, watching his face in the light of an oncoming truck. "And I take it that hasn't happened before? Alma wanting to tell you something, I mean."

"You got that right, though she once did the same sort of thing to Laura, pulled her aside and told her she saw a dark cloud hanging over her just before Laura was diagnosed with cancer. Anyway, Alma grabbed my arm and wouldn't let go. Then she told me that someone—a woman—had just come into my life but that I had to be real careful since she had a secret."

Erica slowly let out her breath. "And you think the someone is me?"

"Well, Alma said a beautiful woman. You fit the bill."

Erica watched as he turned the corner onto the road leading out of town. Rolling the word *secret* through her mind, she felt a tremor go through her. "Everybody's got secrets, Clay," she said, keeping her tone as even as possible.

"I guess I've got things I choose not to discuss with folks," he said, "but I don't know that I've got any deep, dark secrets."

She paused before answering. "Are you asking if I do?"

"It's none of my business, I know, and I don't mean to pry. But to tell you the truth, the reason I brought it up is because I reckon there's a guy involved and I...didn't want to...step on any toes."

"I see." She didn't say anything for several heartbeats. Then she spoke. "I'm not married, if that's what you're wondering. I'm not engaged, either, though I was once. But that ended well over a year ago and I don't have a boyfriend now. I suppose you could say I date casually and have no desire for entanglements."

"Entanglements, huh?"

"I choose not to get seriously involved."

"Because you got burned?"

She gave him an amused smile when he glanced over. "I don't think I said I was burned. I said I was engaged once, and it didn't work out."

"There's usually a reason for that."

"Almost always, I'm sure."

"Which is to say I'm sticking my nose where it doesn't belong again. Sorry." He took hold of her hand then, and drew it to his face, first kissing it, then rubbing it against his cheek. "I'm glad you aren't involved with anyone," he said. "Mighty glad."

Erica's heart raced. And she welcomed the silence that followed.

They left the town and she stared out the side window as they cruised down the dark highway, thinking about what Clay had said. Alma Jones was right, she did have a secret, and this might have been a good opportunity to tell Clay about the hepatitis. It would have been the natural thing to do. But she'd been enjoying herself so much she didn't want to spoil this one night of fun she'd allowed herself, though the time would soon come when she'd have to reveal the truth. But not now, she told herself. Not yet.

THEY'D BEEN SITTING up on the butte for maybe ten minutes, looking at the lights of the town below and talking, when the MacInneses arrived. John pulled up his pickup right next to Clay's. With the windows down, it was practically like they were all sitting together in the same row of seats. Kate handed a six-pack to Clay.

"What's with the kids these days?" John said. "Remember back in our time how this place would be packed like a parking lot, especially after a football game?"

"It's a weeknight," Clay said. "And it could be there's a new spot. One car was leaving as we arrived, though."

"More likely it's that midnight stalker again." John hooted. "The one with the hook."

"Oh, John, honestly!" Kate said. She looked at them, shaking her head. "Sometimes I wonder why I married the man."

"You married me because your daddy found out what it was we were doing up here, sugar." Then he howled.

"John, will you shut up!" Again Kate shook her head. "And he hasn't even had his first beer."

"What station you got on over there, partner?" John said to Clay. "We might as well get some stereo going."

Clay told him, then handed Erica a beer.

"No, thanks," she said. "I don't drink."

"Not at all?"

"No. Liver problem. Doctor won't let me."

"Oh. Sorry to hear that." He looked at the bottle he'd opened as though he didn't know what to do with it. "You should have said something."

"It doesn't bother me if someone else drinks. I'm not an alcoholic or anything. In fact, if you want to drink my share, I'll drive us home. Whenever I go out with friends, I'm usually the designated driver."

"I'm not a big drinker myself," Clay said, "but I have a beer now and again. Sure you don't mind?"

"Not at all."

"Well, why don't you scoot over here so we can be a bit more cozy?" he said.

Erica moved closer and Clay put his arm around her shoulders. She felt herself relax against him. And when he kissed her hair as if he'd done it a thousand times, she sighed.

Clay took a sip of beer, then turned to say something to his friends. He turned back, chuckling, then lowered his voice to a whisper. "Well, look over there," he said, tossing his head toward the Mac-Inneses' truck.

Erica took a peek past Clay's shoulder and saw that John and Kate were kissing passionately.

"Testimony to the fact that it's not necessarily over when you get married, huh?" he said.

She giggled. "No, seems not."

"So, what were you like in high school?" he asked, taking another drink from his can.

"I was rather serious, quiet. I guess I was well enough liked, but I wasn't in the really 'in' group."

"You weren't a cheerleader or prom queen?"

"Nope, but I was an also-ran."

Clay shook his head. "If you lost, I'd sure like to see the winner."

"She's a TV reporter in Chicago now. Terri Walker's her name."

"And you're a big-time consultant."

"Not so big-time."

"By my standards you are," he said.

Erica glanced at him from the corner of her eye. She could tell he was thinking about kissing her again and that made her heart race. Funny, but the whole day had been moving toward this moment. The conversation, the touching, the dancing, seeing the lights of the town by night—it all had been coming to this.

He touched her lower lip with his fingertip, slowly lowering his face toward hers. "You know, I couldn't think of anyplace on earth I'd rather be than here with you at Flat Iron Rock."

"Why's that?"

"Because it's me—the same way the Lone Eagle is me, and those lights out there are me."

She tried to keep the tremor out of her voice, but it wasn't easy because she cared about the answer. "And how many girls have you said that to?"

"Believe it or not, you're the first."

With that, he touched his lips to hers, softly at first, but then with growing force. This time she relaxed at once, opening her lips so the kiss could deepen. Clay seemed to be breathing her in. She felt his tongue flick over her lower lip and the edge of her teeth as his fingers traced her jaw and neck.

She felt a pang of desire, not just a need to be touched and held and kissed, but a craving for more, to be taken, to merge with this man, and she was shocked. She hadn't been intimate with anyone for quite a while. And Clay, well, she'd known that he'd been inching toward this from the first, but in her mind he was only her fantasy cowboy—nothing more than a chance to let down her hair and have fun. Yet something about this, the way he held her, the need she felt, demanded more than a fantasy.

His excitement grew and she realized she had to slow things down. John and Kate were only a few feet away. Even if they were kissing too, she had her pride. Erica broke her mouth away, but their faces remained together, their breathing heavy. It was obvious what might happen if she *really* let go. Sally might have been thinking in those terms, but should she? Could she?

"Flat Iron Rock does seem to have a little magic," she murmured.

"Why do you think I brought you here?" he growled.

She leaned forward and whispered in his ear, "It couldn't have been because you're a gentleman."

He chuckled, then his expression turned serious, his gray eyes glinting. "No, it's because I've wanted to kiss you like this ever since you stopped to give me a lift. And you know it, Erica. You felt it, too."

"I don't know if it was quite that quick with me," she confessed, "but you're right, I felt it."

Clay kissed the end of her nose. "I like a woman who's not afraid to talk about her desires," he said.

Erica suddenly wondered about Laura. In fact, Laura had been in the back of her mind ever since the girl had first been mentioned. Erica knew the impact she'd had on his life and a part of her worried that maybe Clay was using her to revisit old feelings.

Their faces were still close when the mood was broken by the sound of a door opening. They looked over to see John and Kate sliding out the driver's side of his truck. John glanced at them.

"Kate and I are going to take a little walk," he said. "A little walk down memory lane."

It wasn't until the couple moved off that they could see John had a blanket under his arm. The MacInneses soon disappeared over the rocky ledge.

"Are they going to do what I think they're going to do?" Erica said.

"Could be." Clay drew on his beer. "There's a spot just down over the ledge where people would go when they wanted privacy. In the old days, we called it the bedroom."

"My, my," she said, "I guess they *are* taking a walk down memory lane." She turned to Clay and, gathering her courage, asked, "How about you? Does being here bring back memories?"

Erica found herself holding her breath while she waited for him to answer.

"Yes, but I'm not thinking of her, Erica. I'm only thinking of you."

She let out her breath, relieved. But there was no time to think about what Clay had said, or what it might mean, because he kissed her again.

8

WHEN HE FINALLY pulled away from kissing her, Clay ran his fingers lightly down the side of her neck, making Erica shiver. It was amazing, but her body seemed to have a will of its own, caring only for the pleasure of the moment. Was it Clay? Or had she been thinking too much in the past when she'd been with other men? Erica didn't know.

Clay pressed his face into her hair, inhaling her scent. "You smell wonderful," he muttered.

She closed her eyes, savoring the moment. "It's the perfume."

"No, it's the chemistry, the woman underneath that counts."

She pulled back a bit and gave him a puckish smile. "Why, Clay, you're beginning to sound like a man who's been around more than a herd of cattle. Or maybe the setting is bringing back fond memories. Could that be it?"

He grinned back, giving her a squeeze. "Don't you go giving me a bad time just because I find you attractive. You're every bit as responsible for this as I am, Miss Ross."

"Well, you have a point." She sighed. "I suppose my days as a blushing virgin are long past."

"Does being at a place like this bring back memories for you, too?" he asked. "I guess Denver, being so large and all, would have to have several places like Flat Iron Rock."

"Actually, I grew up in Colorado Springs, smaller than Denver, but a lot larger than Red Rock. Our favorite place to go back then was the Garden of the Gods. It's a mystical place, you know. Sacred to Native Americans."

"Complete with ghosts, too. At least that's the way I heard it."

"That was part of the excitement, I suppose. At least, we used to pretend that was a part of it."

"So naturally when a guy drove you up there, he'd have to put his arm around you to protect you." Clay slipped his arm around her and she snuggled close to him once more.

She chuckled. "Yes, I think you've got the idea."

"I don't think we have any ghosts here, but if it would inspire you, I can tell you a ghost story."

Erica traced his lip with her fingertip. "I don't know that you need any help."

He kissed her deeply then, at the same time slipping his fingers through the opening of her blouse. The next thing Erica knew, her blouse was unbuttoned. Her hand was on Clay's jean-clad leg and she felt the taut, hard muscles beneath the fabric as he unfastened the hook at the front of her bra. When he lightly stroked her nipple, her heart began to race.

Moaning, she let her head fall back against the window, allowing Clay room to lean down to suckle her. As his tongue painted a moist patch on her breast, Erica's breathing grew short and labored. The Garden of the Gods had never been like this.

Feeling herself moisten, she drew her hand up Clay's leg until it rested on the bulge at his crotch.

She suddenly hated it that they were in a pickup truck. She wanted to stretch out and feel his body next to hers, her leg against his leg, her stomach and torso against his. She wanted his warmth, but more than that, she wanted the kind of connection she could only have if they were naked and in each other's arms.

Instead, she railed against the confined space. But in a strange way, her restlessness only heightened her desire. The feel of his callused hand on the underside of her breast aroused her; his warmth made her want to burrow closer to him. His scent filled her nostrils and she wanted to inhale him, make him a part of her.

As his lips moved along the side of her neck, sending shivers down her spine, she felt his hand between her legs. She wanted to slip out of her jeans and toss them off. She didn't want anything between his skin and hers. But even that would not be enough to satisfy her now. She wanted him inside her.

Perhaps sensing it, Clay unfastened the snap at her waistband and lowered the zipper. Now only her panties were between her and his fingers. She arched against his hand as he stroked her.

"Oh, Clay," she murmured, her excitement growing more intense. She knew there was no turning back now.

When Clay kissed the corner of her mouth, she took his face in her hands and kissed him deeply, all the while arching her hips in rhythm with his touch. Clay slid his hand under her panties, finding her moist center. The jolt that surged through her was so strong she had to cross her legs, trapping his hand.

"You taste so sweet," he said, his hot breath on her eyes and cheek.

"Clay, if you're out of practice, I can't imagine what it would be like to be with you when you're in practice."

"I take it those are words of encouragement," he said, drawing his tongue up into the little hollow at the base of her ear.

"Let me put it this way. If you stop now, I'll kill you."

"Whatever makes the lady happy." With that, he parted her legs and resumed caressing her, ever so lightly now, more teasing and alluring than forceful. Her legs began to quiver as she closed her eyes, her whole being focused on the tip of his finger.

Her hips began rocking. The rhythm of his caress quickened. When he lowered his head and took her nipple between his lips, she cried out.

"Oh, Clay," she cried as wave after pulsing wave went through her. After a few moments of ecstasy, she drew Clay's hand from her panties. Turning her face toward him, she kissed his chin, again placing her hand on the swollen bulge of his loins. "You certainly do know how to make a girl happy, Mr. McCormick," she whispered. "But then, I guess I already amply illustrated that."

"You're not just any girl," he said, pushing a strand of hair back off her face.

Erica smiled in the darkness. A moment later they heard voices coming from the edge of the precipice. "Oh, Lord," she said, sitting bolt upright.

Erica fastened her jeans, hooked her bra and was buttoning her blouse when they saw the MacInneses appear. Kate was giggling. Seeing the trucks, Kate

smoothed her hair. Erica did the same as she and
Clay exchanged woeful looks.

"That's what friends are for," he said under his
breath. "To keep a guy in line."

"They didn't quite save me," she whispered, now
thoroughly embarrassed.

"Would you have wanted to be saved?"

"Of course not, but I have to say that if I'm going
to maintain the illusion of being a lady."

"You're not just a lady, you're a fabulous lady,"
he said, kissing the end of her nose.

John and Kate had reached their truck. He opened
the door on the driver's side and she slipped into the
seat, glancing over with embarrassment, again fuss-
ing with her hair. "Well, all the same constellations
are still there," she said with a self-conscious laugh.

"Yep," John added. "And we picked out every
one...when we weren't otherwise occupied."

"John!" Kate protested. "You promised, no wise-
cracks."

"I don't reckon Clay and Erica have been sitting
up here discussin' trends in the stock market."

"You'd be surprised," Clay said. "This here's a
city girl."

Erica gave him a jab with her elbow, then leaned
past him. "Kate," she said, "I've got to ask. Would I
happen to be sitting in the truck of the biggest heart-
throb in Red Rock?"

"Clay and this man of mine both had the fathers
of all the girls in Montezuma County buying shot-
guns. And that's the last I'm going to say on the subject tonight."

"Clay, maybe," John protested. "But the only guy
I had on *my* tail was Kate's old man."

"Hey," Clay said. "Some friends you two are!"

"Sorry, sweetie," Kate said, "but you're going to have to defend your reputation on your own. We don't mean to be party poopers, but John and I are going home. To be honest, I feel like I've got ants all over me, and the minute I walk in the house, I'm headed straight for the tub." She gave a little wave. "Nice meeting you, Erica. Hope to see you again soon. Good night!"

With that, her window went up and John started the engine. In seconds they were gone.

Clay watched them go in his rearview mirror. "Poor Kate, you could tell she was dying of embarrassment."

"Little did she know," Erica said, reflecting. "On the other hand, maybe she knew all too well."

"I really wasn't all that bad when I was a kid," he insisted.

"Well, you found time to practice somewhere along the line," she said, patting his cheek. "Or, let me put it this way—you have a knack for a lot more than bulldogging."

He chuckled. Then, taking the ends of her hair between his fingers, he said, "You're quite a bit of inspiration, Erica Ross. A hell of a lot."

They exchanged smiles and kissed lightly on the lips.

"If I'm not mistaken," he said, "your fondest desire right now is to go home and have a hot bath yourself."

"Clay, you're not only a gentleman, you know the female mind."

He brushed her cheek with his fingers. "I try, sweetheart. I try."

CLAY HAD ONLY HAD one beer, but he let Erica drive anyway. For reasons he didn't understand, she'd slipped from playfulness into an introspective frame of mind. It had been fifteen minutes since she'd spoken, her attention seemingly focused on the road, though he could tell something weighty was going on in her pretty head.

"You're being awfully quiet," he said. "What are you thinking?"

"Oh, nothing, really. Just random thoughts." She turned to give him a quick look. "Why? Should something be wrong?"

"No. I guess guys get a little uneasy when a woman gets quiet."

"And why is that? Are they afraid she might be having independent thoughts?"

He blinked, surprised by her tone. "Did I do something to offend you?"

"No, I've had a wonderful time. You're a good dancer and a very sexy man. What woman in my shoes could possibly complain?"

Maybe Erica wasn't complaining, but her words were ringing hollow. Something *was* wrong, he decided. Then he recalled Alma Jones's comment about a secret. He wondered if there might be something to that.

"You know what rule four of the Cowboy Code is?" he asked.

She shook her head. "I have no idea."

"'If you want to dance, it's best to pick a time when the music's playing.'"

"That one makes sense. Why do you mention it?"

"Because I'm fixin' to dance, Erica, and I've got this feeling you just turned off the music."

"I'm tired, Clay. If I'm quiet that's the reason."

His expression was skeptical and she noticed.

"Look," she said, "I'm a high-energy person, but when my tank's empty, I crash."

"With all due respect, I don't think that's what it is."

"I don't mean to be difficult," she said, "but I'd rather not talk about it if you don't mind."

"Suit yourself."

He stared at the dark highway ahead, unsure what had gone wrong. Obviously, he'd done something, played it badly. But in spite of his honest desire to set things right, Erica wasn't helping much. There were times when the best way to handle a skittish animal was to back off and let it be. It was the same with people, he'd found. Especially women.

Suddenly Erica slammed on the brakes for a jackrabbit that was in the middle of the pavement, locked in the headlights. She honked, making the animal scamper off into the sagebrush, then resumed her speed. "It's a wonder they live to multiply," she muttered.

"I think it's called ecological balance," he said. "Rabbits breed and get run over at a stable rate. But once we have that theme park, there'll be scads more tourists and more rabbits will be killed, which'll throw off the ecological balance. Before long, global warming will get worse, the snows will melt and we'll have flood, famine, pestilence, political instability, revolution and war."

She chuckled. "And I can save the world by scotching Julia's ghost-town theme park, is that the point?"

He slowly shook his head. "I never claimed to be subtle."

"I guess not."

Clay let her stew for a while. He'd done about as much as he could to bridge the gap between them. Though he hadn't the slightest idea what had gone wrong, he wasn't going to do all the worrying. As far as he was concerned, she could carry the ball for a while.

After a few minutes, she took the bait. "I know I must seem a little crazy," she said, "running hot and cold, but I want you to know it's not intentional. I'm really at a loss as to what's best."

"What's the problem?" he asked, hoping that she was ready now to say whatever was on her mind.

"A number of things, I guess—like what your expectations are, how this'll seem to me tomorrow, how it'll seem to you. People tend to get carried away when there's a full moon, you know."

"You aren't going to blame what happened tonight on the moon, are you?" he said.

"Of course not. Part of the reason I got carried away is because you were irresistible."

He reached over and toyed with the ends of her hair. "That's what you call it, huh—getting carried away?"

She gave him a quick glance. "What do you call it?"

"Well, we didn't get carried away very far."

"Speak for yourself."

"I admit we know each other a lot better now than when the evening started. Personally, I consider that good...and I hope you do, too."

"I gave myself permission to have a good time,

and I did. You were a great date. My first cowboy, as a matter of fact.''

''But you're not interested in too much of a good thing.''

She took a deep breath before answering. ''That's a very good way to put it, actually.''

He put his booted foot up on the dashboard. ''Might have known.''

When they came to the entrance to the ranch, Erica slowed, making the turn. She was driving carefully, showing a responsible side that appealed to him. She was a woman with a brain. Brave and independent. There was a softness about her, a vulnerability that touched his soul. But there was also a downside. This hang-up, this...secret or whatever the hell it was, that was getting in the way.

They went another mile without a word being said. Before long they came to the ranch house. They passed it, making their way up the valley. Clay's annoyance began to grow. Not that he felt a woman owed him sex—that wasn't the issue. But they did owe a fella honesty, and he was sure as sin that Erica wasn't being fully truthful. Despite her halfhearted assurances to the contrary, she was pulling back, disengaging emotionally, not just physically.

Finally they came to the cabin. Stopping under the trees, Erica set the hand brake, but she didn't turn off the ignition. ''I know you'd like to come in,'' she said, looking directly into his eyes, ''but, at the risk of hurting your feelings, which I really don't want to do, I'm going to beg off.''

''Virtue is its own punishment,'' he said.

''I'm sorry, Clay, I really am.''

"I'd like to know if that's true. Almost as much as I'd like to know what's going on inside your head."

"You can't accept the fact that my feelings are as they are?"

"Sure I can, if I know what the hell they are. Erica, one minute things are going great, the next thing I know you're kissing me off."

"I guess the truth is, I stopped to think about what was happening," she said.

"Well, I'm not one to try to scrape honey from a hornet's nest, so I reckon I'll just have to respect your decision. If I offended you, which I apparently did, you have my apology."

She put her head in her hands. "Let's just drop it. Please."

"That's easy for you to say."

She hesitated only a moment before abruptly opening the door and jumping out of the truck. Clay got out, too, intercepting her before she reached the front door. She tried to move past him, but he took hold of her arm.

"Let's not leave it like this."

She looked up at him, her eyes shimmering. "I don't know what to say."

He stared at her, shaking his head. "Rule six. 'If you've got to choose between ridin' a bull and arguing with a stubborn woman, choose the bull.'"

She peered into his eyes, the moonlight illuminating her face. "Believe it or not, I'm not arguing, and I'm not being stubborn, either. I'm afraid."

He considered that for a moment. "Of what? My feelings or your feelings? That I'll like you too much or not enough?"

She bit her lip, unable to look at him. Clay took

hold of her chin and made her look at him. "Erica, which is it?"

Tears welled in her eyes and started running down her cheeks. It was the one sight he couldn't take. He crushed her against his chest and held her there, stroking her head. She sobbed softly in his arms. He felt terrible for having made her cry, but he still didn't know why this was happening.

Taking her by the shoulders then, he said, "Look, I know I'm making a mess of this, but can't you see that I care about you. I don't want you just walking away without an explanation."

She sniffled and wiped her eyes with her hand. "Clay, I'm sick," she said, her voice quavering. "I didn't want to tell you, but I can see there's no way to avoid it. I'm seriously ill."

"Huh?"

"I have hepatitis C. I was diagnosed a few years ago and I'm...well, it's potentially fatal."

"Hepatitis?" he murmured.

"Yes, the incurable kind."

He was stunned. "But..."

"The fact that I don't have any visible symptoms doesn't mean that the condition isn't serious. My liver is damaged. It's very fragile. I have no idea what the future will bring. I live week by week, month by month."

He was utterly speechless.

"I would have said something earlier, maybe I *should* have said something earlier, but I thought as long as we were just going to be friends...but then...well, I guess it started feeling a little *too* friendly."

"Erica..." He felt dreadful, just awful. It was like

getting kicked in the stomach. A lump formed in his throat. He fumbled for words.

"When I heard about Laura," she went on quickly, "and how she died, my first thought was uh-oh, I've got to be careful. I decided I wasn't going to get involved with you at all, even though I was attracted to you. Then I thought maybe we could have a little fun, and as long as things stayed..." Her voice trailed off and she wiped her eyes again. "It was a mistake," she said. "My feelings were too hard to control. I guess I...started liking you...a bit too much."

She gazed into his eyes, trying to smile but not succeeding. "I know now to avoid good-looking cowboys," she said, putting her hand on his chest. "I'm so sorry. So very sorry." Then, getting up on her toes, she kissed his cheek. "Good night. Thank you for the wonderful evening. I wish it didn't have to end this way...for both our sakes."

He was still too stunned to move. He wanted to embrace her, but all that pain and trauma from the past, the deep, abiding sorrow, came rushing into his heart, a nightmare revisited. Erica slipped away then, leaving behind her soft scent and a yawning, aching void in his heart.

ERICA LAY IN HER BED, crying silently as the moonlight washed over her. She was reliving the worst moments with Tom all over again. The only difference was, this time she'd pulled the trigger first, saving Clay the trouble.

She was sorry now that she'd encouraged him, sorry she'd gone with him, sorry she'd allowed things to become intimate, sorry she hadn't told him she was ill right up front. The problem was that she'd wanted to experience a fun, carefree, romantic evening with him. And she'd picked the worst possible guy at the worst possible time. Clay was much more than just a cowboy date. He liked her as much as she liked him. And, because of Laura, he was vulnerable. She'd lured him out of his shell, only to be hurt and disappointed.

At least she'd stopped things before they'd gotten serious. Any damage she'd caused him probably wouldn't be permanent, though it was likely that Clay might not venture out with a woman again anytime soon. Lord knew, she'd learned the hard way how difficult it was to be hurt, and then take a chance on facing pain again. Erica really only dated to remind herself that she wasn't dead yet. She always held back a part of herself—although it wasn't easy.

She didn't know what she would have done if Clay had insisted that he didn't care about her illness. She'd dated a few guys who didn't think it was a big deal, but then, they weren't particularly serious about her. She had a feeling Clay was—or at least he was headed in that direction. When she'd told him, he'd gone into shock. It was déjà vu for him, the poor guy. The expression on his face had said it all.

Erica felt worse for him than she did for herself. She'd grown used to holding back. And she'd known going in that whatever they did, it had to stop short of serious involvement. That wasn't true in Clay's case. The fact that sex wasn't the issue almost made it harder. She would have been able to live with it so much more easily if all he'd wanted was to spend the night with her. But he wanted more. It was in his eyes, his voice, the way he touched her. How had she let this happen? And what was she going to do about it now?

9

AFTER BREAKFAST the next morning Erica drove up to the house to work with Julia. She figured Clay would be long gone—which turned out to be the case—and that he wouldn't have said anything to his grandmother—which was also apparent.

Erica wondered if she should tell Julia about her illness, if and when the topic arose naturally in conversation, or if she was better off to keep it to herself. As to what had happened between her and Clay, she'd leave it to him to tell Julia if he chose. She considered that more his business than hers.

"So, what did you think of Red Rock?" Julia asked as they sat down to talk.

"It's a nice little town and I loved the Cowboy Club."

She sighed wistfully. "In so many ways that place was my life."

"I can see why."

"But it's better for me not to look back on it so nostalgically," Julia said. "I don't know if you can understand this, but it's hard for me to go there sometimes."

"I do understand."

Julia drifted off into her memories for a few minutes, then brought herself back to the conversation. "I trust you and Clay had a good time."

The image of the two of them up at Flat Iron Rock flashed into her mind, making her feel the color rise to her cheeks. "Clay is a nice man, a very nice man," she replied, not quite able to look into Julia's eyes.

"Yes, but he's set in his ways. It's defensiveness, though. He's had his share of pain and doesn't want to endure more."

Julia's words added to Erica's own pain, and her regret. "I understand that very well."

Julia studied her, weighing the comment, then apparently decided it was up to Erica to elaborate, if she wished. But Erica simply couldn't bring herself to go into it now, the anguish of the night before was a bit too fresh.

"So, my dear," the woman said, "what's next?"

"I'd like to talk to the county-government folks," Erica replied. "Infrastructure, services, permits, fees and the like are going to be critical to a project like this."

"I know everybody at the county who matters, so I think it's best if we drive over to Cortez together so I can introduce you personally."

"Great. It always helps if doors are open."

"The staff types are all on our side. We'll have problems with a couple of the elected officials, but I think a majority will vote our way when it comes to that."

"On a big project, politics almost always is the bottom line," Erica said.

"That's one battle we'll probably win."

"So, we could have a winner...if it makes financial sense."

"And you're the one to tell me that," Julia said.

Erica smiled politely. They were talking about her

life's work, but she found herself unable to generate much excitement. Clay, and their emotional parting, consumed her thoughts.

But she forced herself to get some work done that day, reading the documentation she'd accumulated. She took extensive notes and Rosita kept her well supplied with coffee. Over lunch, Erica and Julia decided to drive to Cortez, the county seat, that afternoon. Julia telephoned to make sure that everybody they needed to see would be around.

Erica wasn't surprised that Clay didn't show up for lunch, but she was curious about his state of mind. So when she carried her lunch dishes into the kitchen, she took the opportunity to ask Rosita what kind of mood Clay had been in that morning.

"I didn't see him, *señorita*. Señor McCormick and my husband and some of the men, they left at dawn and are gone for two or three days to move the cattle from the mountains. A busy time is coming for them."

Apparently, Clay had shaken off whatever disappointment he'd felt and had thrown himself into his work. At first Erica was disheartened, then she realized his absence was probably a good thing. In fact, it was a very good thing. Not having to see each other and deal with the embarrassment was better for them both. If Clay was willing, which she figured he was, they wouldn't have to see each other for the balance of her stay, particularly if she had her dinner at the cabin on days he was around.

THE TRIP to the county offices that afternoon went well. Julia had the ear of every official they spoke with, and the planning department was forthcoming. Erica left with the county development plan, an armload of maps, aerial photos, environmental studies and enough data to occupy her for a week. On the way back to the Lone Eagle, Julia, who was driving her big Lincoln, took a detour to see Luke Calloway, a rancher about Julia's age and one of the county commissioners unlikely to support the project.

"Trying to overwhelm me with beauty, are you, Julia?" he said when she introduced Erica.

"Luke, if I thought for a moment you were referring to the both of us, I'd go with you to the Autumn Roundup this year. But since I know you weren't, I'm going to have to turn you down again."

"Julia, of course I was referring to you." Calloway, a big, barrel-chested man, laughed. "I expect Miss Ross has already caught the eye of the young scallywags like that grandson of yours."

"Too late, Luke. Your only recourse now is to look favorably on my theme park, if and when it comes up for a vote."

"Julia, you wouldn't be tryin' to bribe me, would you?" he said with a satyr-like grin.

"I'll leave that to your imagination, Mr. Calloway."

With that Julia said her goodbyes and led Erica back to the car. They were soon off with a wave, leaving the rancher on his porch, hands on his hips, looking after them.

"You seem to have his number," Erica said admiringly.

"God only knows if it'll do any good," Julia replied. "But it's the only way I'll ever get to the old goat. Luke's been chasing me ever since his wife died six years ago. But the fact remains, these old ranchers vote with their wallet first, their heart second and their conscience last."

"Is Clay that way, too?" Erica didn't know why she'd brought him up, but it just slipped out.

"Yes and no. Clay loves the Lone Eagle, but for sentimental reasons more than for the wealth and income it represents. He might be the exception."

Erica remained silent as they drove along. Julia did, too, but after a while she ventured a comment.

"You must have put a dent in his bumper last night," she said.

Erica turned to her. "What do you mean?"

"Clay cleared out of the house before sunup."

"That's what Rosita said. He's on a roundup."

"Yes, dear, but it wasn't scheduled for another week. All I know is, he gathered up the boys and they took off for the hills rather suddenly."

"Maybe it's because of the weather or something."

"I'd say more likely you."

Erica felt herself blush, but she couldn't exactly deny Julia's words. "I think Clay and I have an understanding," she finally said.

Julia paused for a long moment before she spoke. "I hope you let him down easily."

Erica sighed. "As easily as I could." She wanted to tell Julia it had hurt her as much as Clay, but that would only complicate things. Better to leave matters as they were. She could bear responsibility, as well as pain. They were both a big part of her life and probably always would be.

THAT EVENING Erica had dinner with Julia. Relations between them remained cordial, even warm, but Erica could tell the woman was disappointed she'd turned Clay off. Several times Erica almost said something about her illness, knowing that would explain everything, but she didn't want that issue injected into their business relationship if it wasn't necessary.

"Julia," she said, wanting to keep things focused on the project, "I think it's time I have a look at the site."

"I've been thinking the same thing," Julia said. "I know it's important. I'd intended to discuss it with Clay, but he took off so quick I couldn't. The thing is, I'm not sure if you could get in there with an off-road vehicle, or if it would be necessary to go by horseback. Do you ride, dear?"

"Yes, but not particularly well."

"I learned well enough to keep my husband happy and to accompany him when it mattered, but my heart was never in it. Haven't been on a horse since the day he died."

Erica regarded her. Julia seemed to be one of those women who had made hard choices in life and then had lived in peace with the bargains she'd made. She had given up her career for the man she loved, then had done her very best to put her own stamp on that life. Erica wondered whether she'd have done half as well if she'd been given the opportunity to make Julia's kind of choices.

"Out of curiosity, what keeps you here, Julia?"

"Love. And need. I loved Hap and I loved our life together. After that it was the Cowboy Club. Then Kiley and Clay needed me. I don't know if Clay needs me now—on balance, I suppose he doesn't—

but I love the boy and this is the only home I've had for over fifty years. I go back to California for a visit every year or two, but I must tell you, the place has left me far behind. I live a quiet life here, sometimes I think too quiet, but I like the clean air, the low stress and the friendly people. Thank God for my VCR and my books, though."

It was interesting to Erica to hear Julia philosophize. They were of two different generations, but there was an odd kinship between them. Both were independent women who'd suffered loss and overcome adversity. They were survivors and doers. Erica took comfort in knowing she had older sisters who'd blazed the trail for her generation.

Still, when she drove back to the cabin that night, she was very much aware of her loneliness. Before going inside, she stood on the porch for several minutes and stared up at the moon through the cottonwood trees. Twenty-four hours earlier she'd been sixteen again, fantasizing a little about falling in love with a sexy cowboy. But Clay was gone now. Sure, she had some wonderful memories—Clay McCormick's brand was on her heart. But her soul yearned for more—more of him, more of the kind of love fate had decreed was not to be.

CLAY NEEDED TO BE ALONE so he left the campfire and moved through the trees onto the spur protruding from the mountainside. He found a gently rounded boulder that afforded an unobstructed view of the plains to the south and west, and sat down, pulling the collar of his sheepskin coat up around his neck. Washed in the silvery moonlight, the landscape spread before him was a muted canvas of sepias, beiges, blacks and grays. The lower hills prevented him from seeing the lights of the ranch house, but he knew exactly where it was. He knew where the cabin was, too.

He couldn't think about Erica without pain stabbing his gut. The woman who'd seemed so vital and strong had, in the passing of a moment, been transformed into a frail specter, an elusive shadow. How could a man hold on to something so tentative, so easily lost? How could he trust in something as fragile as another's life? When he'd tried to do that with Laura, the wind had seemed to pick up their hopes and dreams and carry them away as he watched, helpless. Now Erica's life was being threatened. The saddest part was, there wasn't a damn thing he could do about it. There was no dragon to slay, no sacrifice to make.

Erica wasn't exactly dying, but as sure as he gave her his heart, she would. He was cursed that way. Sure, that might not be a scientific fact, but it was hard to ignore fear when it was lodged in your emotions, lurking in a place where logic failed. Death was a slippery devil, especially when the death concerned somebody you loved.

Erica Ross wasn't Laura, of course. But even though they had just met, something told him she could be. Things had moved that quickly. Damned if the first woman he'd let himself really care for since Laura didn't turn out to be touched by the same sort of tragedy. He didn't need to go through that again. It wouldn't serve her and it certainly wouldn't serve him.

Yet, sure as he wanted to run away from her—run from the pain—part of him wanted to hold her in his arms, protect her. But loving her would mean risking the loss that would surely come. There was no middle ground. He either stayed clear of her, or he embraced the problem with his very being, giving everything he had to give.

As he listened to the faint strains of the country-and-western tune coming from the radio that one of the boys had brought, he heard someone calling to him.

"Hey, boss!" The voice was coming from the woods behind him. "Boss, you here?"

Clay could tell it was Emilio. "Yo," he called. "I'm out here on the rock."

A minute later the foreman emerged from the woods. "Sorry to bother you, but Julia called. Sounded like she wanted to talk to you pretty bad."

Clay wondered what it could be. Chances were it was urgent because she almost never called him on the cell phone when he was out on the range. He didn't much care for the intrusion of technology into the life-style he'd cut out for himself, but it was common sense to take advantage of the convenience.

Even so, he didn't personally lug the damn thing unless he was out alone. He made Emilio or one of the boys pack it.

Clay got up and clambered down off the rock, meeting Emilio at the base of it. The phone was in Emilio's hand.

"Julia didn't say what it was about?"

The foreman shook his head. Clay took the phone from him.

"Okay, thanks, I'll call her."

Emilio nodded and headed toward camp. Clay weighed the instrument in his hand, sensing it wasn't a conversation he was going to like. He punched in the number of the ranch, then touched the send button. Julia answered on the second ring.

"Thanks for calling back," she said. "I'm really sorry to intrude. I know how you hate being bothered when you're out under the open sky."

"That's all right, Gram, what's up?"

"It's Erica," she replied.

Clay's stomach sank. He'd figured that was it.

"She needs to see the movie town," Julia went on. "Examining the site is very important. I didn't know whether there's enough road left that she could get there in the Jeep or if she needs to ride in by horseback. I'd intended to talk to you about it, but you left so suddenly this morning…"

"Yeah, I forgot completely about that," he said, relieved that it wasn't something more serious.

"I would have waited until you got back, but Rosita said it could be as long as three days or more before we saw you."

"That's all right, Gram. I should have talked to you before I headed out." He paused for a moment to reflect. "I don't think it's a good idea to send her out on her own, even in a four-wheel. You should probably have Monty drive her. Assuming the road's no worse than the last time I was in there, they might be able to make it through. The sure way, of course, is to go by horseback. Does she ride?"

"I think about as well as I used to, Clay, which, as you know, isn't so hot."

He sighed. "Have Monty drive her then, but tell him not to take any chances. If they can't get through easily, I'll have to arrange something else…I don't know what, maybe fly her in by chopper. But it'd take a while to set that up."

"Yes," Julia said, "I think the Jeep is the best bet. I'll talk to Monty in the morning."

"Make sure he knows it's a one-day excursion. If they head out at sunup they should get in a full day of exploration and still be back by dark. What, exactly, will she be doing there?"

"She wants to get a bunch of photos for one thing, evaluate the condition of the buildings for another."

"All right, then. She should be able to get a lot of that done in a day."

"Thank you so much, Clay."

"No problem, Gram. Everything else all right?"

"Fine. How about with you? Cattle look okay?"

"Real good."

"That's nice."

Clay figured she must have been able to tell there was something else on his mind—either that or she wanted to say something more herself. He decided the best thing to do was hit it head-on. Being coy in a cell-phone conversation was silly.

"How is Erica, anyway?" he asked.

"Fine."

"Fine?"

"Yes. Why shouldn't she be? The more relevant question is, how are *you?*"

"There's not a damn thing wrong with me, Gram."

"Oh? I would have thought differently."

Clay was confused. Then it occurred to him that Erica might not have spoken to her, at least not frankly. He decided to proceed cautiously. "Why would you have thought differently?"

"I suppose it's none of my business."

"We're already talking about it, so you might as well consider it your business," he said.

"Maybe *you* should tell *me* what the problem is, Clay."

"Gram, have you talked to Erica?"

"Not in detail, but I gather your...friendship is...in hiatus."

"That's one way to put it, I suppose." He was beginning to realize that Julia didn't know the details. Erica might not even have told her about her illness.

"How would *you* put it?" she asked him.

"Friendship between Erica and me doesn't seem to be in the cards," he replied. "That's about as blunt as I can put it."

"I think that's a shame. Not that it's really any of my business. You're both adults and can make those kinds of decisions for yourselves. But Wanda said...oops...uh...there I go again, talking out of turn."

"Wanda said what, Gram?"

"Wanda said you looked so cute together and that she hadn't seen you looking so happy in years."

Clay pretty near came right out and asked her if Erica had discussed her health with her, but realized it wasn't his place to broadcast that sort of thing. "We had a good time," he said, "but that hardly means we're going to have a relationship. Erica's here to do business with you, Gram. That's her number-one priority and I've got priorities of my own. So, can we leave it at that?"

"Certainly. You don't owe me any explanations."

Clay was uncomfortable with the way the call had gone, but this wasn't the time for a heart-to-heart talk with his grandmother. They said goodbye and he disconnected the call.

Damn, he thought as he began trudging back toward camp, why did women have to be so confounding? It'd be so much easier for everybody if they were more like men.

ERICA WAS PROPPED UP in bed, reading, when she heard a vehicle. Wondering who it could be, she checked her watch. It was nearly 10:00 p.m. Then it occurred to her—it was probably Clay.

She quickly got out of bed and put on her bathrobe. She didn't have time to get dressed. It didn't matter. People couldn't expect her to look as if she was ready for a night on the town at this hour. Thank goodness she hadn't washed off her makeup.

Running a brush through her hair, she left the tiny bedroom and got to the front door of the cabin just as there was a knock. To show she wasn't a complete fool, she asked who it was before pulling the door open.

"It's Monty Evans, ma'am, the assistant foreman of the Lone Eagle. Mrs. Sommers asked me to bring you a message."

Erica's heart sank. She was so sure it would be Clay, though she had no idea why it would be, or what he would have said. She opened the door.

A lanky, horse-faced ranch hand stood self-consciously in the door, his hat in his hand. Monty Evans appeared to be in his late forties. It was the first time she'd seen him. "Begging your pardon, ma'am," Monty said, handing her a slip of paper, "but Julia...er, Mrs. Sommers...wrote this here note for you."

Erica took the note from his hand, and partially turned to the light so that she could read it.

Erica,
I talked to Clay by phone and he suggested that the best way to get to the movie town was by Jeep. Monty will drive you, but you'll have to leave at the crack of dawn in order to have time at the location to do what you need to do.

   If you'd like to go tomorrow, tell Monty, and the two of you can decide on the hour, etc. Rosita will send along lunch and snacks. Dress for the heat and rough country. Monty can relay any questions to me.

                                    Julia

Erica looked at the man. "Yes, tomorrow morning's fine. What time do you want to pick me up?"

"Six too early, ma'am?"

"No, six is fine."

"I'll be here then."

"Thank you."

"Yes, ma'am."

He returned to his truck and Erica closed the door. Leaning against it, she told herself this was good. Seeing the site was, of course, essential in the evaluation of any project. But she couldn't stop herself from feeling disappointed that she wouldn't be going with Clay—despite knowing that being around him at all was a bad idea. They both had far too much baggage. Besides, some things were simply not meant to be.

LATE THE NEXT MORNING Clay, Dibs Cutler and Steve Fernandez were moving a small herd out of a draw toward the main body when Emilio came riding up the shallow creek, full tilt. He was sweating, his eyes round with urgency as he pulled up next to Clay.

"Boss," he said breathlessly, "there's been an accident. It's Monty. He was taking Miss Ross to the ghost town in the Jeep and he turned the sucker over. Thinks he broke his leg."

"What about Erica?" he asked, a sudden terror raging in his heart.

"I guess she's okay. Maybe some bumps and bruises. She called Mrs. Sommers on Monty's cell phone and Mrs. Sommers called me, maybe five minutes ago."

Clay heaved a sigh of relief. "You have the phone?"

Emilio took the phone from his pocket and handed it to him. Clay dialed the ranch-house number. Julia answered right away.

"Gram, how bad is it? Was Erica hurt?"

"Not so far as I know. But Monty can't walk and the Jeep's turned over. Erica's got him in the shade and she's giving him water. I didn't know whether I should call the sheriff or what, Clay."

"Where are they, exactly?"

"Monty said they got most of the way through the canyon to within a couple of miles of the town."

"That's what I was afraid of. I reckon it'd take a rescue unit a couple of hours to get there, minimum. We're only an hour away. I'm going to take a couple of the boys and pick them up. If we can bring him out in the Jeep, we will. Otherwise, it'll have to be by horseback. Does Monty think he can ride?"

"I imagine so. He asked me to send some horses."

"We're closer, so leave that to me. Call him back and tell him we're on our way. And, Gram, have an ambulance waiting at the top of the Old Springs Road. Doesn't sound serious enough for Medevac."

"No, Monty didn't even want me calling you. He was really embarrassed."

"But you're sure Erica's okay?"

"She bumped her head and her elbow, but says she's fine. Mostly she was worried about Monty."

Clay wasn't surprised by that. The woman had pluck. But it killed him to think of her hurt and stuck out in the hot sun. It couldn't be doing her hepatitis any good, either.

"Clay?"

"I'll look after her, don't worry, Gram."

"She's a sweet girl. Be nice to her."

"I will, Gram. I don't know any other way to be."

10

ERICA PRESSED a damp cloth to the bump above her temple. Other than the dull pain throbbing in her head, she was fine. Monty wasn't complaining, but it was obvious he was in pain. She'd already given him four aspirin from the first-aid kit, which he said helped, but she doubted it. Fortunately, it wasn't a compound fracture. The contusions looked pretty nasty and there was a lot of swelling, but he hadn't bled or gone into shock.

"Would you care for some more water?" she asked.

"Thank you kindly, ma'am. Maybe I would."

Erica handed him the canteen and the man took a long drink.

"My, that tastes good," he said. "Nothing like water when you've got a thirst."

"I'm so sorry this happened," she said. "I take full responsibility."

"No, ma'am. I should have known better than to try to get around that boulder. The boss warned me not to press it, and I did."

"At my insistence."

"Never you mind."

"No," Erica said, "I will mind. I'm going to tell Clay exactly what happened."

"I don't rightly think it'll make no difference. I was responsible."

"Leave it to me," she said.

Monty Evans took out his pocket watch. "I'd say they'll be arrivin' anytime now. I don't reckon it'd be none too soon, neither."

Erica gazed up at the walls of the canyon rising above them on either side. As they'd driven up the road, Monty had told her a number of ambushes had occurred in this very canyon, by Apaches and bandits—of the Hollywood variety, of course. His own father, he'd said, had been an extra in a couple of films shot in the 1940s, once as an outlaw firing down on a wagon train from the rim of the canyon, and once as a prospector in a bar scene. "Pa was prouder of that than the silver buckles he won doin' rodeo," he'd said.

Erica could see that there was movie lore everywhere, and everybody seemed to have a story to tell. She was beginning to appreciate the possibilities for Julia's theme park and better understood her enthusiasm. At first she'd worried that the woman's motive was more a desire to relive the glory of the past than to exploit a commercial opportunity. But now, being out and about, she was starting to see the possibilities, and she still hadn't even checked out the town.

One idea that had occurred to her already was that visitors could be brought to the movie town by wagon from a parking facility at the foot of the canyon. They could stage attacks by outlaws along the way, much as it was done at Disneyland.

But her enthusiasm had been dampened by her concern for Monty. Getting the poor man medical attention was the top priority. Yet she still wanted a firsthand look at Julia's ghost town. Dare she ask Clay if it would be possible to continue by horse-back? she wondered. The idea of seeing him at all had her feeling uneasy, mostly because she knew the encounter would be strained.

Clay clearly wanted nothing to do with her, which was completely understandable. And she told her-self that she felt the same, for his sake, as well as her own. Still, their own sensitivities were secondary to dealing with the crisis at hand. With any luck, they'd hardly need to speak. She certainly intended to make it as low-key as she could.

"I think I hear horses," Monty said, relief on his face.

Erica listened, but at first she heard nothing. Then, after several moments, she heard it, too—the sound of pounding hooves. It grew louder. She got to her feet. A hundred yards up the canyon she could see three horsemen approaching, a cloud of dust kick-ing up behind them. They had two additional horses with them. It seemed odd when she stopped to think about it, but the riders were actually coming to save them, just like in the movies!

Erica waved to get their attention, and the men veered over to the bushes, where she and Monty had taken refuge from the sun. They were a good fifty yards from the overturned Jeep, the closest shade. The men pulled up their horses, the dust cloud slowly drifting off. They'd been riding hard and they were as sweaty as their horses, which were pretty lathered up.

As she watched, Clay dismounted and hurried to-ward them, a frown of concern on his face. He seemed so rugged, manly and in control. Erica couldn't help staring. In his element, he was again that cowboy she'd first encountered on the road.

"So, how many casualties?" he said easily, his expression softening, his tone clearly meant to be reassuring.

He looked at her first, but when he'd apparently assured himself that she was in one piece, his gaze shifted to Monty Evans.

"Think I busted my leg, boss," Monty said. He lifted himself to his elbows as Clay squatted next to him. The injured man slowly shook his head. "Sure am sorry to cause all the trouble."

"It's entirely my fault," Erica interjected, moving forward. "I made him go on when he didn't want to, Clay. I take full responsibility for the accident."

"Hear that, Monty?" Clay said. "The lady's claiming responsibility for your driving."

"Yes, I am," she insisted. "If you're going to blame anyone, blame me."

Clay pushed his hat back on his head and squinted up at her. "Nobody's blaming anybody, Erica," he said. "Ultimately I'm responsible for what happens on this ranch, so I'm as much at fault as anyone."

Erica stood a little straighter. "Thank you, but that's not true. I refused to go back when Monty wanted to stop."

"I reckon what matters at the moment is getting Monty out of here," Clay said. "And you, too. I understand you've got a few bumps."

"I'm fine."

"She got a goose egg on her head where she bumped it, boss," Monty said.

"It's nothing," she insisted.

Clay stood. Taking her face in his hands, he turned her head so he could see the bump. He examined it carefully, gently touching the edge of the wound with the tips of his fingers. "You got thumped all right. And you're going to have a nasty bruise. Your head hurt?"

"Not very badly."

"Hmm."

Erica was aware of his proximity, his manly smell, the mat of hair at the opening of his shirt. She could feel the heat of his body and her skin was extra sensitive where he had touched her. She recalled all the other places those hands had touched—the things he'd done to her body, and she shivered.

"Shame we can't get any ice on it," he said.

She swallowed hard and forced her voice to be even. "I think we need to worry about Monty, not me."

Clay gave her an uneasy smile, his white teeth gleaming in the sun. "Are you hurt anywhere else?"

She shrugged. "I whacked my elbow. But I'll live."

Clay nodded curtly, then pulled away from her to kneel at Monty's side. As soon as his attention had shifted to Monty, she felt bereft. In spite of the heat, the place where his hand had touched her almost seemed cold. She took a deep breath and told herself she had to get control.

Meanwhile, Clay examined Monty's leg. "No question it's broken, partner. And climbing up in a saddle won't help. Let's hope we can get the Jeep running." He stood and peered in the direction of the disabled vehicle, which the others were already inspecting. "How does it look, Dibs?" he called, his voice echoing around the walls of the canyon.

"Can't see nothing wrong with it except it's upside down," the man called back. "Guess we'll know when we get it turned over."

"Reckon that's the first order of business," Clay said as much to himself as anyone. Then, leaning over, he clasped Monty's shoulder. "Take it easy, partner. I'll go have a look at the Jeep. Let's hope the three of us can get it back on its feet."

"I'll help," Erica offered.

Clay shook his head. "No. You might get hurt worse than you already are."

"I'm not hurt. At least not much," she said, miffed. "Since I'm responsible, the least I can do is help."

He gave her a long hard look. She saw the lines around his mouth harden before he spoke. "All right. I suppose you're the best judge of what you're up to doing."

They started walking toward the overturned Jeep. About halfway there, Clay took her arm and, turning to her, said, "I can't help being concerned about you. A bump on the noggin and this hot sun aren't a good combination. And you're just feisty enough to hide some other injury."

"Feisty, am I?"

"I'd say so."

They stared into each other's eyes, each perhaps reliving the emotion of a couple of nights earlier. The sadness she thought she'd expunged came back with a rush. She did her best to shake it off.

"Well, if being independent and self-reliant is

feisty, then maybe I am," she said after a moment of silence.

"That's all well and good, but I don't want you jeopardizing your health."

"Clay, I've got a virus and a damaged liver," she said. "I'm not quite at death's door. At least not yet. As long as I'm feeling well enough to do my work and live my life, that's exactly what I intend to do."

He frowned, letting go of her arm. "It's not my place to tell you what to do. That wasn't my intention."

"Just forget it," she said. "Let's worry about Monty."

"Fine, but I want you to know I care about your well-being, whether you believe that or not. You're not just another person, Erica. In fact, you're pretty damn special." He drew his callused fingers lightly along her jaw, gazing deeply into her eyes. "I hope that doesn't offend you."

She felt tears coming, much to her horror. She didn't cry, but her eyes bubbled and she had to wipe her cheeks, first with the damp handkerchief, then with her sleeve. "Come on," she said, marching off. "Let's see to this Jeep."

The other men watched her coming toward the overturned vehicle. She said hello. Clay came up behind her and introduced her to Dibs and Roy. Both men touched the brims of their hats.

"Well," Clay said, regarding the Jeep, "now all we have to do is flip this baby over."

They appraised the situation. A rock slide had wiped out the trail. Monty had tried to bypass it and the outer wheels had hit unstable soil on the edge of the dry creek bed, which gave way. When the Jeep rolled, Erica had been thrown clear, but the vehicle had landed on Monty's leg. Fortunately, he hadn't been pinned under it.

"I reckon we can roll it back over if we can get leverage," Clay said. "Let's give it a try."

The three men got a grip on the Jeep. Erica grabbed hold of the fender. Clay gave her a look, but didn't admonish her, seeing she was determined.

"All right, on three," he said. "One...two... three!"

The four of them strained, lifting the vehicle most of the way, but their footing wasn't good and they had to let the Jeep drop.

"Let's throw a couple ropes on it and use the horses," Clay said. "No sense breaking our backs."

While the men readied the horses, Erica and Clay took a breather. Removing his hat, he wiped his sweaty forehead with his sleeve. "You sure you should be doing this?" he asked.

"I'm fine, Clay. Really."

He watched the men maneuvering the horses. "There's something I'd like to say," he said. "I've been ashamed of the way I reacted to your news the other night. Frankly, you caught me by surprise. I was stunned. I didn't mean to be thoughtless or impolite."

"Don't be silly, Clay. It's not like it's never happened to me before. If anything, I regret having put you through it."

"Judging by what you said, I figured you wanted space. So that's why I took off. But I may have sent the wrong signal. What I want is to do what's best for you."

"Thanks, but I'd really rather not talk about it. I

have a very simple philosophy. I try to live my life and not dwell on problems. So forget it. Forget the other night, forget me. It's better for both of us."

"Okay, boss," one of the men said. "We're ready."

Clay excused himself and went to the Jeep. "Pull the ropes taut, we'll go on my signal."

Dibs and Roy took the reins of their horses and pulled the ropes taut. Then, when Clay gave the sign, they urged the horses on. The Jeep slowly lifted, finally flipping over and landing upright. The men whooped. While Roy removed the ropes, Clay hopped into the vehicle and tried the engine. It started, eliciting another cheer.

Erica approached and Clay smiled at her, saying, "Now we can get Monty to the hospital and you back to the ranch."

When she frowned, he asked why.

"Monty said we're within a couple of miles of the ghost town. Is that right?"

"Yeah, I'd say two miles or so."

"Would you be willing to loan me a horse so I could ride on up and check it out?"

Clay turned off the engine. "Erica, these are stock horses, cutting horses, not riding-stable horses."

"I'm not a complete novice."

"Yes, but how would you find your way home? And what if you got thrown or the horse took a spill?"

"I'm not an expert, but I *can* ride. And I'd simply follow the trail back to the fork that branches over those hills to the ranch. You don't have to be a genius to follow a well-marked trail. There are two ruts most of the way, for heaven's sake."

Clay looked off, drumming his fingers on the steering wheel.

"I can see you don't like that idea," she said.

"Frankly, no, I don't."

"Okay, fine. They're your horses. Forget I asked. It was probably a stupid idea anyway. I just wanted to do my job, and I'm so close, it's a shame not to be able to see the place."

Clay sighed with exasperation. Erica was sorry now she'd opened her mouth. Turning, she headed back toward the clump of bushes where Monty rested. Behind her, she heard the engine of the Jeep come to life again. The next thing she knew, Clay had pulled right up beside her, rolling with her as she walked.

"You sure are independent," he said.

She gave him a look. "You know what your problem is, Clay? You're used to herding cattle and breaking horses and having a bunch of men at your beck and call. A responsible adult woman, someone who doesn't call you boss, is unfathomable to you."

"Oh, so that's what it is. A gender thing. And I suppose the fact that I'm concerned about your welfare is irrelevant?"

They'd reached Monty, and Clay stopped the Jeep. Erica turned to face him, her hands on her hips. "If I hadn't told you about the hepatitis, would you insist on babying me this way?"

"Probably."

"Well, you're worse than I thought," she huffed.

His eyes narrowed. "What would you prefer? That I ignore you?"

"That's not funny, Clay."

"I don't mean to be funny. I'm just trying to understand you. It seems the nicer I try to be, the madder you get," he said, climbing out of the Jeep.

"I'm not angry," she said, knowing Monty was listening, though she didn't care.

"Then would you care to explain?"

"All I want is to be allowed to go on with my life in peace."

Dibs Cutler came over, making further conversation impossible. Monty looked relieved. Clay turned his attention to the men.

"You up to a nice bumpy ride, Monty?" Clay asked.

"Reckon if I wait for them to put a freeway through, this leg'll have turned to gangrene, boss."

Clay chuckled, shaking his head. "I'd say you're ready. Dibs, give me a hand and we'll lift him into the back of the Jeep."

As they were putting Monty into the Jeep, Erica gathered up her things. She handed Monty the canteen. Roy joined them.

"Okay, here's the plan," Clay said to the gathering. "Dibs, you ride on back to camp and take one of the extra horses. The bay, not the Appaloosa. Roy, I want you to drive Monty to Old Springs Road. There should be an ambulance waiting there to take him to the hospital. Then drop the Jeep at the ranch. Take your horse so you can get back to camp."

"What're you going to do, boss?"

"I'm taking Miss Ross on up to the ghost town. Dibs, tell Emilio I'll get back to camp as soon as I can."

"Clay," Erica said, "I'm obviously interfering with your work and that wasn't my intention. I wanted a horse, not a guide."

"Well, you're getting both. And I'll get to watch a professional consultant at work. You wouldn't mind that, would you?"

She could see he was determined. And though in a way it annoyed her, a part of her was secretly pleased. She refused to let it show, however. "Frankly, I'd feel guilty taking you from your work."

"I can handle your guilt," Clay said, rolling his tongue through his cheek.

"Oh, in that case I feel so much better."

Clay shook his head. "Okay, *city* girl, if you want to be so danged independent, why don't you go get that light-colored horse with the speckles on its haunch and bring it back here?"

"Yes, I know, the Appaloosa."

He raised his eyebrows. "You ever seen one before?"

"No, but I'm a quick study, *country* boy."

With that, she turned and walked away. She'd noticed a few raised eyebrows. The men obviously weren't used to hearing Clay talked to that way, by anyone. She figured it was about time.

SHE WAS A BETTER RIDER than he'd expected, and not afraid to assert herself with the horse. The first few minutes he kept his eye on her, watching her every move in case she had been more severely injured than she'd let on. But other than the bump on her head, and the elbow she'd bruised, she seemed to be okay. Eventually he relaxed and let her be. And though he gave her a tip now and then, mostly he let her learn from her mistakes. He could see she was proud and spirited. Between that, her intelligence and her beauty, he kept forgetting about the hepatitis C—and the fact that he *shouldn't* be thinking of her in those terms. Erica Ross was off-limits, same as if she was married or engaged. Not that it made things any easier.

Considering his growing obsession with her, and the undeniable attraction he felt, Dibs should have been the one to take her to the old movie town. But then, he never had been the kind of man who necessarily did what common sense dictated.

That was a problem in this situation. He cared about Erica, more than he'd have thought possible considering how briefly he'd known her. Lord knew, he didn't want to hurt her, and that meant he had to respect her wishes. The decent thing was to show her compassion. He certainly felt compassion. Too much.

Erica had made it clear that a relationship was as much of a problem for her as it was for him. And yet, the firmer she was, and the more she ignored him, the more he wondered if she wasn't protesting a little too much. One thing was certain. The more she ignored him, the more he wanted to interact with her.

It wasn't long before they came out onto an open plain. Dead ahead, perhaps a mile away, the rooftops of the ghost town could be seen, gray against the ruddy-brown mountains.

"Is that it?" she asked.

"Yep, that's Julia's movie town."

He saw a flicker of excitement at the corner of her mouth and she leaned forward slightly in the saddle. "It looks convincing enough from here."

"Most of the buildings were made sturdy. But

they're mainly empty shells since they were used for exterior shots," he told her.

"For somebody who hates Hollywood, you seem to know the lingo."

"Growing up, I heard all about the movie business. But I don't hate Hollywood, Erica. I just like it right where it is."

"Have you been to the ghost town often?" she asked.

"To spend any time, maybe twice. But I ride through fairly regularly, just to make sure everything's okay. I do recall my first visit really well, though."

"What happened?"

"It was when Kiley was little. Gram brought the two of us out here to see 'her town,' as she called it. First, though, she had us watch a couple of old movies that had been shot here, so we'd recognize things when we saw them. We had a ball. I climbed up on rooftops where bad guys fell from after being shot. And of course, we went into the saloon. That was one of the few buildings that was finished inside. I got to stand right where Gary Cooper and John Wayne had their gunfights."

"That had to be exciting for a kid."

"It was one of my fonder memories, I must admit."

"That wouldn't have anything to do with why you don't want it to become a theme park, would it? You don't want to ruin those memories, I mean."

He smiled, liking that she understood him well enough to know what was in his heart. If he had to guess, Erica was the kind of woman who would always understand what he was truly thinking and feeling. "I'd be lying if I didn't say it was a factor. But I reckon you already got that one figured out."

Clay was glad she'd loosened up some. Maybe she'd decided that since she was going to be stuck with him for a few hours, there was no point in being unfriendly.

"Tell me, Clay, are all cowboys afraid of change, or is it just you?"

"I don't know that change is the issue so much as not liking for things to get in the way."

"What do you mean?"

"This is a hard life in many ways," he explained. "We're always facing challenges. To win the struggle you have to be focused, determined. Rule nine of the Cowboy Code goes like this—'Climbing in the saddle's easy. The hard part's staying in it until you get where you're going.' Determination and perseverance are essential, Erica. A cowboy can get irritated at a fly buzzin' round his head. People with ridiculous ideas are sort of like flies."

"Ridiculous ideas like ghost-town theme parks?"

Grinning, he said, "Your words, not mine."

"Maybe your horizons are too limited," she said.

"Think that's my problem?"

"Maybe."

"So, do you think you could broaden them a little, if you had a mind to?"

"That almost sounds like an invitation, Clay—or a challenge, I'm not sure which."

He had a terrible urge to lean over, grab her and give her one hell of a kiss. Damn if she didn't affect him that way, even as her very existence tore at his heart. "How do you feel about challenges?" he asked.

Then Erica did something he hadn't seen her do yet that day. She laughed. "Clay, you're a crazy cowboy, you really are."

"Why do you say that?"

"I don't know, you have a knack for disarming the opposition."

He grinned. "Oh, you're the opposition, are you? We've gone from opponents to friends and back to opponents."

Their eyes met and she laughed again, moved, obviously, by some secret amusement. "I'll say this about you," she said, "it's hard to stay mad at you."

"I think it's because we both have a competitive spirit."

"You think *I'm* competitive?" she said. "Me?"

"I think women love nothing better than challenging a man. They don't particularly like beating him, but they sure do like getting his dander up."

"Clay McCormick, that's the most sexist comment I've ever heard."

"I'll prove it. You said you weren't hurt. But are you up to galloping that pony a little?" he asked.

Her eyes sparkled. "You mean have a race?"

"Why not? Unless you're afraid."

"Clay, you are *so* transparent."

"It's less than half a mile to that church building," he said, pointing. "How much of a head start do you need?"

"You'd be lucky to beat me if we started even," she said.

With that she gave her horse a sharp kick in the side. It broke first into a gallop, then a dead run. Erica gave a little shriek, though he wasn't sure if it was out of fear or excitement. He took off after her.

They were nearly to the church before he managed to pull up alongside her. Her horse went full tilt, she bounced all over the saddle, her eyes round as saucers.

"You all right?" he shouted over the thunder of the hooves.

There were no words on her lips, but her eyes were full of desperation. He reached over and grabbed the reins of her horse, bringing her to a halt at the church building.

"Oh my God!" she said, clutching her hand to her breast. "I didn't know a horse could run that fast!"

The horses spun around, kicking up dust, and it took a while for Clay to get them under control.

"I thought if you gave a horse a kick, it was supposed to gallop," Erica said, catching her breath.

"A spirited quarter horse will take liberties," Clay told her. "You look like you got bumped around some. Want to get down?"

Erica nodded, apparently not willing to let her pride get in the way of her comfort. Clay dismounted, then helped her off her horse, half catching her in his arms. Though she was hot and her face was speckled with dust and perspiration, she had the same sweet smell as when they'd danced. She stared into his eyes a long timeless moment before extricating herself, staggering a few steps away.

"You okay?" he asked. "You didn't get jarred too much, did you?"

"I probably won't be able to walk for a week."

"I shouldn't have suggested we race," he said. "I took the teasing a bit too far."

"It would have served us both right if I'd broken my neck."

He move a little closer, a frown of real concern on his face. "Heavy exercise isn't bad for you, is it?"

She shook her head. "No, but I have to be careful not to overdo it. Mainly it's stress I have to avoid."

"Then you're okay?"

She chuckled. "Clay, I'm fine. Quit worrying, will you?"

"All right. I won't." They were simply words. How could he not worry? How could he not care?

They were in front of the church. Like the rest of the buildings, the boards were weathered gray. A heap of tumbleweed was piled against the side of the structure.

"So, that church is fake, huh?" she said.

"Yep, just a prop. Doesn't even have a floor. Gram used to say what's real about the movies is what you feel. The rest doesn't matter."

"Did you buy that?"

"Yes, but there's a different kind of reality that's even more important."

"Which is…"

"Those mountains," he said, gesturing. "This land, the sky."

She nodded. "And staying in the saddle no matter what the threat."

"Guess being transparent has its downside," he said, chuckling.

"You're nothing, Clay, if you aren't consistent."

"I don't reckon that's something I need to apologize for."

"I suppose it's not."

They began walking slowly up the empty wind-blown street, lined with wooden buildings of various sizes and shapes. She took it all in, he assumed with the eye of a project analyst.

"Is that a cemetery?" she asked, pointing to the hillock at the far end of the street.

"Boot Hill," he explained. "And there's a hanging tree up there around the corner. Neither real, of course."

Erica stopped, glancing around. "I should take pictures," she said.

He helped her get her gear from the saddlebags. She had notebooks, maps, aerial photos, documents of various kinds, even some basic drafting equipment. Clay suggested she set up shop in the saloon. The door was padlocked. He opened it for her.

The inside was stripped bare, the floor and other surfaces were thick with dust. But the bar was intact. Clay led the way, pushing through the cobwebs. He dusted off a section of the bar, using his sleeve.

"That should help some," he said.

"It's great, thanks."

"How long do you think you'll need?"

She laughed. "That's a little like asking a kid how much time they want to spend in a toy store. Maybe I should ask how long you're going to give me."

The afternoon sun angled in the open door, illuminating her face. He felt the same feeling he'd had before, when he was kissing her up on Flat Iron Rock. Unable to help himself, he reached out and brushed her cheek with the back of his fingers. "Wisp of cobweb," he said. It wasn't true.

Erica lowered her eyes. "Can I have a couple of hours?"

"Sure. I'll water the horses or ride on up to the

guest house to make sure no varmints have broken in."

"Guest house?"

"That's what Gram always called it," he told her. "One of the studios got permission from my grandfather to build a little house for producers and studio executives and folks like that who'd come to visit the set. They didn't want to have to stay in a trailer like the crews. Occasionally a big star would stay there, especially if there was another big star around that he or she was especially friendly with. When Gram brought my sister and me here, the three of us stayed there. Most of the furniture is gone. I'll bet nobody's stayed in it for twenty years. I've been intending to check it out, but have never had time to do more than ride by."

"Where is it?"

"On the other side of Boot Hill. Quarter of a mile from here."

"Well, I have plenty to keep me busy," she said.

"Then it's high time I get out of your way."

She nodded. "See you later."

"Watch yourself, Erica. Don't step on any rattlesnakes or anything."

Her eyes narrowed. "Clay McCormick, you could have gone all day without saying that."

He chuckled. "My liability carrier told me I should be sure and warn people."

"Get out of here!"

Laughing, he turned and sauntered out the door.

11

SHE'D GONE THROUGH three rolls of film, photographing every building from every conceivable angle. She'd done it systematically so that she could correlate the pictures to the aerial photographs. The schematics she had with her turned out to be approximate, so she'd added detail and rough measurements. She'd also checked out the structure of the buildings and found that Clay was right. The construction was sound, but the majority were only shells.

Erica figured most of them could be finished and turned into shops, restaurants, handicraft centers and historical displays, much like Williamsburg in Virginia. In fact, the more she saw of the ghost town, the more convinced she became that a park with authenticity and historical integrity might have more marketing appeal than a simple amusement facility. The Old West and the Hollywood connection in combination might have potent drawing power.

Erica had spotted a ladder built into the rear of the main group of attached buildings and decided to go to the roof to get a higher perspective of the street and Boot Hill. Slinging her camera over her shoulder, she climbed the ladder, realizing before too many steps that she was a lot more sore from the Jeep accident and the horseback ride than she had thought. But she had a job to do, and so she crossed the roof to the front of the building, picking her way carefully. In addition to having a good perspective on the town from this vantage point, she had a nice view of the high mountain plain that, to the west, stretched for miles unmarred by civilization. It could have been the 1880s as readily as the 1990s.

The sun, she noticed, was beginning to drop low in the sky. Checking her watch, she saw that she'd been at work for nearly three hours. The time had gone quickly, even with occasional lapses into melancholy reflection about Clay. The poor guy was thinking of her in ways that were dangerous for them both. And yet she couldn't bring herself to condemn him, even in her own mind.

When he'd touched her face her insides had gone soft and it was all she could do to keep from touching him back. How tempted she'd been to just let herself drift into his arms. How she'd have liked for him to hold her—just hold her. If she thought it would stop at that, she'd have let it happen. But she knew they both wanted more, a lot more. So she told herself that she'd have to be strong for both of them, even if it was painful.

Erica knew she'd let herself be distracted long enough. Pulling her camera around, she began snapping pictures of the street and the surrounding terrain, carefully referencing each shot in her notebook, which she'd set on the railing. As she made her last entry, she saw that Clay was in the street, right below her. He was on his horse, his right leg wrapped around the saddle horn. He peered up at her from under the brim of his hat, looking sexy as hell.

"How long have you been sitting there?" she called out.

"Just a couple of minutes. I've been trying to figure out what you're doing."

"No movie stunts, I assure you. Just taking pictures and making notes." She saw he had the Appaloosa ready and waiting. "I suppose you've come to tell me it's time to go."

"Unless you want to make the trip by moonlight. As it is we'll be doing the last few miles in the dark."

"I hate the thought of getting back in the saddle again." She rubbed her sore elbow. "But I have gotten a lot done. The time got away from me."

"It got away from me, too. You'll never believe what I found up at the guest house."

"What?"

"Several photo albums with shots of moviemaking during the forties and fifties, scrapbooks and even a guest register with the names of famous stars, directors and other movie people. Gram once told me all that stuff existed, but she'd lost track of it. I found it all stacked in a kitchen cupboard."

"Julia will be thrilled."

"Yeah, there's some pretty neat stuff. But I decided rather than try to lug it back, I'd get it later, either when I had a pack animal or a four-wheel drive."

"So, I guess I better come down."

"Unless you want to walk home by yourself."

Erica gingerly made her way to the rear of the building. She had stiffened up some, and it wasn't easy to maneuver. She was halfway down the ladder when she paused to shift her camera bag. That's when she noticed Clay there, waiting. "You plan on catching me if I fall?" she asked.

"Yes, as a matter of fact."

She descended the last few rungs, dropping to the ground with a groan. Turning, she dusted her hands, giving Clay a look of amusement. "You're just sure I'm going to break like a China doll, aren't you?"

He gave a half shrug.

"Clay, I won't. Believe me."

"I guess I do have an overwhelming...I don't know, compulsion, I guess...to be protective."

"Fortunately for both of us, I'm not yours to protect."

He stared at her a long moment, then said, "I don't see that as being especially fortunate."

Seeing his eyes glisten, she realized she'd been too brusque. She'd hurt him. "I'm sorry," she murmured. "That was insensitive. Please forgive me."

Clay grimaced. He was clearly fighting his feelings. "I wish you weren't quite so good at this," he finally muttered.

"Good at what?"

"Good at putting things aside. Good at pretending we can't be more than friends. Good at being able to look right through me like I was a window."

"Clay, it's not that way at all. I've learned to protect myself out of necessity."

"Maybe you don't need to protect yourself, Erica."

She felt emotion surging in her. She searched for a way to explain, to reassure, to plead, to beg. All she could think to do was run.

"We should go," she said, hurrying past him before the tears began to flow.

Erica went inside the saloon and gathered everything up. When she went out front, she found Clay waiting with the horses. She hardly glanced at him, because she knew if he caught her eye she'd break down. There was only one way to deal with temptation, and that was with firmness.

As he mounted his horse, she started packing her notebooks and camera in the saddlebag.

"Need help?" he asked, his voice soft as the wind.

"No, thank you."

She stood there, looking at her horse, thinking of how stiff and sore she felt, and for the life of her, she couldn't force herself to put one foot in the stirrup and swing her leg over the saddle.

Clay regarded her, probably wondering why she was just standing there. His gaze was intense. "So, how's your butt?" he finally asked.

"Good enough to get home. I guess it has to be."

"Not necessarily."

She looked up at him. "What do you mean?"

"We could stay at the guest house tonight. There's not a lot there for comfort, but it wouldn't be like sleeping on the cold ground."

Erica frowned. "I think that's a very bad idea."

"I cleaned the place," he said. "I even got the pump working, so there's water."

"You planned this," she said, accusation in her voice.

"No, ma'am. Initially I was just going to take you over to show you what I found. I had time to kill, so I started cleaning. Us staying did go through my mind, but I didn't decide to come right out and suggest it until I...well...I guess you could say, noticed that you aren't too thrilled with the idea of a long ride back."

She let out a long sigh. "It shows?"

"Yeah. You looked so darn pretty up there on the roof—sort of like Juliet on her balcony. But when you started to climb down, well, you seemed to be sort of stiff."

"You can say that again."

"I'm not trying to come on to you," he said quickly. "I'd enjoy being with you, sitting by the fire. That's all. I care about you, Erica, and I'd like to be alone with you."

"Even if I stay, I'm not going to be intimate with you again, Clay. You might as well know that right up front." She took a deep breath. "I wouldn't have the other night except that the situation sort of sneaked up on me."

He didn't say anything for a full minute. When he finally did speak, his voice was low and soft. "Don't be afraid of me, Erica."

She gritted her teeth, all set to deny it. Then she decided not to bother. He wouldn't believe her anyway. "Okay, you win. I'll admit it. I *am* afraid. And you should be, too."

Tears began to form. She could hardly bear to look at him and see the emotion in his eyes. She couldn't stand the pain of impossibility. There was resignation in his eyes, disappointment, but no bitterness, no anger. He said nothing, nor did she.

Clay patted his horse with gruff affection, the carelessness of the gesture a contrast to the finesse with which he'd made love with her. She stared at him, her heart swelling. She wanted so badly to be weak, to give in to her desires. But to admit it was to invite disaster.

The sun was dropping rapidly now. She told herself they probably wouldn't be able to get through the canyon before dusk anyway. She thought of the treasures at the guest house. She glanced at him again, this man of the land who tamed horses but couldn't tame his own soul.

"Just tell me this," she said. "Does this guest house have a place where I can wash my face? I can't tell you how dirty and gritty and sweaty I feel." The words rushed out of her like a bird fleeing a cage.

Clay took off his hat, scratching his head. "There's a basin and a tub, but I'd have to lug in the water from the well out back. There's no electric pump or generator to make it work. And the water won't be warm."

"If negative selling is your game, you've sold me. I'll stay. But don't you dare be a bastard and gloat," she warned, shaking a finger at him.

"If I'm a bastard, rest assured I'm one of the gentlemanly variety." He pushed his hat back and creased his forehead. "I do have a serious question though. In fairness, I should ask it now."

Her heart fluttered. "Okay. Shoot."

"This hepatitis you've got. Is it like you're going to die for sure in three years, five years, ten years…whatever?"

A lump formed in her throat. "No, but it's possible. More likely I won't than I will. Especially if I take care of myself."

Clay nodded. "Okay."

He moved his horse forward so that he was right next to her. Erica reached up and touched his hand to get his attention. "Wait a minute. What do you mean, 'Okay?' What if I'd said the odds were very strong I'd be dead in five years? What would you have said then?"

He gave her that crooked grin of his. "No different."

"Then why did you ask?"

Clay squeezed her fingers. Erica stared into his mystical gray eyes. "I asked because I wanted to know," he said. "I don't like surprises."

WHILE CLAY CARRIED water from the well, Erica wandered around the guest house. She ended up at the old table in the main room, where Clay had left the photo albums he'd found. Sitting on one of the three straight chairs, she spent a few minutes leafing through the albums.

All the upholstered furniture had been removed from the house. In one of the bedrooms there was an old iron bedframe but no mattress. Clay had left his bedroll at the camp, but he'd found four sheepskins in the attic, a tarp and several old sheets that had been used to wrap paintings. He'd shaken everything out real well, getting rid of most of the dust. All those items, plus the saddle blankets, would make a fairly comfortable pallet, he'd told her.

"You obviously haven't heard the story of the princess and the pea," she'd said.

"Oh, I heard it when I was a kid," he replied. "I just never could figure out what difference a pea would make."

"Clay, you spend too much time sleeping on the ground."

He'd laughed and given her a kiss before bringing

firewood in from the shed and stacking it in front of the stone fireplace. "This has to be the best-seasoned firewood in recorded history."

Erica had felt a certain exhilaration at the thought of setting up house with Clay, even though it was only going to be for one night. Though neither of them had said a word about it, there seemed to be an unspoken agreement between them—they would enjoy the evening for what it was and let tomorrow take care of itself. No more warnings or recriminations. No more defenses.

And though a huge part of her liked that, there was a corner of her that felt…well, nervous. Given her condition, they couldn't have unprotected sex and she was sure sex was on his mind—as it was on hers—despite what he'd said. She would have to say something to him, but she also had to find the right time.

The lunch Rosita had made was sitting on the corner of the table, still wrapped in plastic. The thought of it made her mouth water because she hadn't eaten since breakfast. While she'd waited with Monty, she'd nibbled on carrots sticks and oatmeal cookies, but that was it. Though she was hungry, she'd told Clay she absolutely had to get cleaned up first.

She was looking at some photos taken on the set of a western when Clay came into the main room, setting the empty bucket by the door. "Your bath's ready, milady," he said. "I hope you've got a little Swedish blood in your veins. The water's cold."

"I don't care if it's icy. I feel so grungy the tub could be full of polar bears and I'd get in."

"The soap and hand towel from my trail kit's on the basin."

Clay had shown her the towel earlier. She had tea towels that were bigger. "How can you dry yourself off with that thing?" she'd asked.

"It's fine for your face," he'd said. "If I take a bath, I either dry off in the sun or in my clothes, depending on how cold the air is."

"Men are basically barbarians when there's no woman around," she'd said. "I see that now."

He'd laughed, something he'd told her he didn't usually do so much. She made him happy, he'd said.

Clay came over to the table. Standing next to her, he looked down at the album, flipped a couple of pages, then pointed to a group photo that appeared to be taken in front of the ranch house. "See anybody you recognize?" he asked.

Erica peered at the picture. The sun had set and the light coming in the window was getting faint. She pointed at the tall middle-aged woman in the center of the group. "Is that Julia?"

"Yep. How about the tyke standing in front of her?"

She looked closely. "Clay, is that you?"

"Age five. The younger woman next to Gram is my mother. The man next to her, my father. The others are family friends. It was Gram's birthday. My mother organized a party. One of my earliest memories of a social occasion."

Erica studied the photo. "You were darling."

"Earnest, I guess."

"Are those little cowboy boots you were wearing?"

"I was born in boots, sweetheart."

She shook her head.

"Hey, maybe you should take your bath," he said. "No point in letting the water get warm."

Erica gave him a whack on his rock-hard stomach. "Smart-ass."

She got to her feet. Clay reached out, gathering her by the waist and pulling her against him. "How about a last taste before you become irresistible?" he said, sinking his face into her neck.

"Yuck," she said, halfheartedly pushing him away. "I feel like sweaty sandpaper. Wait until I'm cleaned up." She headed for the bathroom.

"Don't forget to save a little soap and water for me," he called after her. "And I'll have a fire going to help dry you by the time you're through."

She hurried to the bath. The stub of a candle that Clay had found in the kitchen was burning on the basin, casting a faint glow over the room. His little hand towel was folded neatly over the tub and the bar of soap from his kit sat atop it. His thoughtfulness touched her.

She stripped out of her clothes and lifted one leg over the side of the tub. Dipping her toe in the water, she nearly yelped. It was so cold, it was painful. She put her foot in the rest of the way and then brought the other one in, as well. When she squatted, goose bumps formed on her arms and shoulders. Her teeth started chattering. Figuring she'd die of exposure if she didn't hurry, she frantically soaped herself, even dipping her head in the water and washing her hair.

After rinsing herself, she snatched up the thin little towel, but it was soon soaked. She felt miserable but clean. The miserable part was most notable at the moment. "Clay McCormick," she screamed, "I hate you!"

She heard laughter from the other room.

"I do! I swear!"

She was still trying to dry herself off when she heard his boots on the wooden floor. It sounded as if he was headed toward the bathroom. She flinched, nearly dropping the towel in the water. Surely he wouldn't come walking in!

He didn't. He knocked instead.

"W-w-what?" she said through chattering teeth.

"How would you like one of these sheets to wrap around you so you can sit by the fire and dry off?"

"O-o-okay," she said, stepping out of the tub. When the door started to open, she shrieked. "Wait!" she cried, jumping behind the door.

"No need to be modest when you're living in a state of nature," he said, laughing.

"Speak for yourself," she said as a disembodied hand holding a half sheet came in the door. She snatched the sheet from him. "Thank you. You can leave now."

"You don't need help drying off?"

"Go!"

Clay went off, chuckling. "You wouldn't have made much of a pioneer, sweetheart," he called to her.

"No, I'd never have left Boston," she yelled back, greedily wrapping the thin sheet around her. It smelled of dust, but she didn't care.

Hunched over the basin, Erica rinsed out her underclothes and hung them on the towel bar. She was reluctant to go out with nothing on but a sheet, but she didn't want to get dressed without drying off and warming up. So, wrapping herself up tightly in the sheet, she padded into the front room.

A fire was blazing. Clay was at the table, setting out the food Rosita had prepared that morning. Erica went to the tall fireplace.

"Oh, heaven," she said, feeling the warmth. Opening the sheet, she held it behind her with outstretched arms, using it as a screen while exposing her body to the heat of the fire. The warmth on her skin felt fabulous. "Thank you so much for the fire, Clay," she said, glancing over her shoulder.

She noticed him contemplating her.

"I hope you aren't having nasty thoughts," she said.

"Nasty, no. I was thinking of the shadow puppets I used to play with as a kid. I'd put on shows in front of the fireplace for Kiley. She loved 'em."

Erica realized with horror that she was putting on a shadow show of her own and she was the puppet. "Oh my God," she gasped, dropping to the floor where she sat hugging her knees, the sheet pulled taut around her. "How embarrassing!"

"I don't know if anybody's ever told you, Miss Ross, but you've got a hell of a figure."

"Stop it, Clay! Can't you see I'm humiliated?"

"No reason to be. I'm impressed as hell."

She buried her head in her arms, shaking it. "Don't you have to go get cleaned up or something?"

"Ah, eager to see my puppet show, are you?"

"Clay McCormick, I don't want to hear another word about this. Ever!"

Chuckling, he went off, sheet in hand. Erica was deeply embarrassed, but also flattered. Clay's playfulness pleased her. And he seemed to have put aside any angst he felt over her illness. Was he repressing it for the night, or had he truly come to terms with it? Perhaps he was ignoring it—living for the moment. She wanted to think so. Lord knew, that's what she was doing. Today mattered, not tomorrow.

She thought again of her original notion of a summer romance, meeting somebody and having a fling. Was that still possible with Clay, despite his sad history? Or was she kidding herself? Ironically, it was up to him much more than it was up to her.

Realizing she was wasting a valuable opportunity to dry her hair, Erica crawled closer to the fire and, after tying the sheet under her arms, lowered her head and briskly worked her hair with her fingers. After a minute she heard Clay singing. That struck her as funny, even though he actually had a rather nice voice.

When she stopped to think about it, the whole situation was preposterous. Here she was, off in the wilderness with a cowboy who was singing in the bathtub. Wouldn't Sally get a hoot out of this?

After a few minutes, her hair was reasonably dry and so was she. Getting her hairbrush from her purse, she brushed out the tangles, glad there wasn't a mirror so she'd know just how dreadful she looked. There hadn't even been one in the bathroom.

The sheet was damp, making her long for clean, dry clothes. She'd left her jeans and blouse in the bathroom, but didn't relish putting them on anyway. There wasn't a lot of choice, though. Once Clay came out, she'd get them and dress. By morning, she figured, her underwear would have dried out.

After another few minutes, Clay returned to the

front room with his sheet tied around his waist. It hung to his ankles. His hair was wet, his broad chest bare, though covered with a mat of dark hair. He approached the fireplace unashamed, exuding sex appeal, as masculine and confident a man as she had ever seen. Erica, despite her own modesty, was a bit awestruck.

Clay had what appeared to be wet laundry in his hand. "Are you dry?" he asked, gazing down at her.

She smoothed her hair with her fingers, knowing she looked awful. "Dry but bedraggled. Mercifully there's no mirror. But I am going to get dressed."

"I think your underthings are still wet. And I took the liberty of washing out your blouse along with my shirt," he said, indicating the bundle in his hand.

"Clay, what am I going to wear?" she said anxiously.

"Hang on, I thought of that." He went to the chair where he'd draped his saddlebags, returning with a clean work shirt. "When I'm out on the range for a couple of days, I carry a change of clothes. You can use it as a nightshirt, if you wish," he said, tossing it to her.

The blue denim shirt was wrinkled, but it was clean and soft from all the washings it had been through. "What are *you* going to wear?" she asked.

"The shirt I washed out should be dry in a few hours if I hang it by the fire." He brought one of the chairs over near the fire and hung both his shirt and her blouse on it. Then he sat down next to her. "Aren't you going to put the shirt on?"

"Not in front of you."

"Want me to turn around?"

"No, thank you," she said, giving him a look. "I'll

go to the bathroom." It was only then she noticed the blood on his jaw. There was another nick on his chin. "What happened to your face?"

"I tried shaving with my knife. I didn't want to look like a barbarian."

She shook her head. The poor thing. She'd shamed him and he'd damn near killed himself trying to impress her with his grooming. "You obviously don't carry a razor on the trail."

"Normally I don't run into beautiful women wearing nothing but a sheet when I'm out on the range," he said with a wry smile. "Special circumstances call for special measures."

"I'm changing," she said, getting to her feet.

She padded off. Once she was away from the fire, the air felt cool. She knew she wouldn't be dallying. Clay had extinguished the candle in the bathroom, and dusk had come and gone, but there was enough light coming in the window above the tub to see shapes. She took off the sheet and hung it on the hook behind the door. Then she put on Clay's shirt. The cuffs came past her fingertips and the tail almost to her knees. It was clean, though, and it felt good on her skin.

Erica returned to the front room. Clay had laid out the sheepskins in front of the fire and was sprawled out, warming his bare feet on the flames. She came and knelt next to him, careful to pull the tail of the shirt down over her thighs. He looked up at her, his head resting on his hand.

"That shirt's never looked so good," he said. "But I really like what's under it."

There was lechery in his grin. She'd seen the same

expression the first minute she'd laid eyes on him. That was Clay.

Reaching out, he took her hand, playing with her fingers. "You know, I can't think of a place I'd rather be, or a person I'd rather be with."

His words, though sweet, sent a pain of anxiety through her. And in spite of the fact that she didn't really want to break the mood, she had to ask. "But is this wise?"

"Is what wise?"

"Are you just dismissing what I told you the other night?"

His expression turned serious. "Are you?"

"I've learned to live with it. And I do that by concentrating on today and whatever I happen to be doing."

"I like that approach," he said, drawing her fingers to his mouth and kissing them. "I think I'll do the same."

"But…"

"But, what?"

"But for me, it's essential. You don't have to live like that."

"Well, maybe I want to," he said. Then, getting to his knees beside her, he lifted her chin with his fingers and kissed her lips.

When he pulled away, Erica lowered her eyes. God, how she wanted to believe that! But deep in her heart, she was also afraid that just today wouldn't be enough.

12

CLAY WATCHED HER finish the last of her sandwich. He didn't know when he'd enjoyed seeing a woman eat nearly as much as he enjoyed watching Erica Ross. There was so much about her he liked—loved even—that it was hard not to be obsessed with her every look, her every gesture. He could stare at her for hours and be content.

That she was only inches from him and wearing nothing but one of his shirts didn't make keeping his hands off her easy. Only his respect for her kept him from taking her into his arms and making love to her. But there was something more important than his attraction, strong though it was. He wanted to connect with the woman within. He wanted to know her soul.

"Mmm," she said, licking her fingers. "I knew I was hungry, but I didn't know I was that hungry."

"It's the exercise and the air," he said.

"Not to mention that I haven't eaten since breakfast."

"That might have something to do with it," he allowed.

Erica stared into the fire, her knees drawn to her chest, her arms wrapped around her legs. Clay had a terrible urge to touch her feet, kiss them.

Rising from his reclining position, he wadded up

the plastic wrap his sandwich had been in and tossed it into the fire. It flared and burnt in seconds. Wearing his jeans now, but still bare-chested, he scooted close to her. They stared into the fire together.

"Can I ask you something, Clay?" she said.

"Sure."

"What do you want? I mean *really* want."

"Are we talking about tonight? I hope we are, because I'm not thinking about tomorrow."

"Yes," she said. "Tonight."

"I want what you want."

She paused for a heartbeat. "Let me rephrase the question. Do you think you could want what I want under *my* terms and conditions?"

"I have a hunch we're negotiating, sugar, or do I read you wrong?"

"I'll be blunt, Clay. We can't make love without protection. Because of the virus I've got, it would be irresponsible. For your sake."

"So, if I happen to have a condom in my wallet, you'd feel okay about it?"

"Is making love with me that important?" she asked.

"Being with you is important, Erica. I can just kiss you or hold you. It can be like the other night up on Flat Iron Rock, or we can sit here telling campfire stories until we fall asleep."

She rested her chin on her knee and stared into the fire. He could see her eyes glistening. "Let me make a confession," she said finally, her voice barely above a whisper. "I came to Red Rock half intending to have a fling. My friend Sally and I joked about it.

A summer romance with a cowboy. Nothing serious." She sighed. "Just my luck, I meet you."

"I reckon by your tone there's something bad about that."

"Clay," she said, turning to him, her eyes shimmering, "you're not just a cowboy. You've been hurt. You loved Laura and lost her."

"Which makes me somehow…unacceptable."

"I saw the look in your eyes when I told you I had a potentially fatal illness. It was déjà vu, and you can't deny it."

"Let me ask you something," he said. "Why didn't you fight the idea of staying here with me tonight? Oh, I know you're sore. Between the Jeep accident and the ride, you've got to be. But you aren't so bad that you couldn't have made it back."

She bit her lip. "You're right. I guess, at some level at least, it's because I wanted to pretend you were that faceless cowboy who could look back at tonight and not care."

"But now you're having doubts. What did I say that sent up all the defenses?"

"Nothing."

"Come on, Erica," he said, touching her hair. "Something happened. If it wasn't me, then it was you. Did you discover that you weren't as tough as you thought?"

"I guess," she said, sniffling.

Clay stroked her head. He felt a strong well of emotion, a well of love. Seeing the bump on her temple where she'd hit her head, he leaned over and kissed it lightly.

"Damn you, Clay," she said, her voice almost a whisper. "I was fine until I met you. Why couldn't you have been a plain old cowboy who just wanted to have a good time—no conditions, no past, no future, nothing but the pleasure of the moment?"

He grinned as he pushed a strand of hair back off her cheek. "I think I've proved I can have a good time. I've got no conditions and I'm all for pleasure."

"That just leaves the past and the future," she murmured.

"You claim you've got the future under control, right?"

"Yes."

"Then I've got a proposition for you. You deal with your future and I'll deal with my past."

"Seriously?" she said.

"I'm tough enough. The question is, are you?"

She gave him a little jab in the side with her elbow, smiling. "Clay, everybody knows that when it comes to the really important things, women are much tougher than men."

"Care to prove it?"

"Kiss me."

He didn't need to be asked twice. Taking her into his arms, he kissed her deeply. They fell back onto the pallet of sheepskins. She put her arms around his neck and Clay ran his hand up under her shirt, over the curve of her hip to her narrow waist, drawing her to him. They kissed passionately and hard.

After a minute she came up for air. Clay smiled as he cupped her breast. He was excited, his erection so firm it hurt. "Want to hear rule seven of the Cowboy Code?" he asked huskily.

"Okay, what's rule seven?"

"'Never make a lady ask twice.'"
Laughing, she pulled his face back down to hers.

ERICA WATCHED HIM unbuckle his belt, lower his zipper and push his jeans down over his hips. He was facing her, his back to the fire, his muscular thighs silhouetted by the brightly burning fire.

As his pants dropped below his knees, she stared up at his shadowed face. She could barely see his eyes, but she sensed his wolflike stare. The fire cast a golden corona of light around his shoulders.

Clay stepped out of his jeans. For several moments he stood there, unashamed, unafraid. Erica began unbuttoning her shirt. She did it slowly, making him wait. The last button unfastened, she pushed each flap off her breasts in turn, allowing the fire to light and warm them. He stepped toward her, dropping to his knees at her side.

Her heart beating rapidly, she reached out, taking his sex in her hand. The tip was as soft as the shaft was firm. She began to stroke him, recalling the care and finesse with which he'd aroused her that night in his truck. The thought of that, and the feel of him in her hand, fueled her excitement.

Though he'd scarcely touched her, she felt his desire. She wanted his vitality, the pleasure of his strength. She would take his body in lieu of his soul because she wanted what was safe.

"Where's the condom?" she whispered.

It was in his clenched fist. He held it out and she took it, removing it from the package. Looking up into his eyes, she took his sex into her mouth. His head rolled back on his shoulders and he groaned.

After a moment or so she put the condom on him, rolling it up his shaft. Then she slowly lay back on the pallet, staring up at his face as her heart raged. "Now please, Clay," she said. "Now."

He moved over her, straddling her with his hands and knees, his face above hers as they peered into each other's eyes. She saw his hunger, but there was something else as well, something soft and frightening. Something that could only be called love.

"I want you inside me," she insisted, fighting her fear. "Please. Quickly."

Clay kissed her mouth. He kissed her neck and breasts. He kissed her belly and drew his tongue up the insides of her thighs. Her body trembled as badly as it had when she was in the tub, but she wasn't cold now. She was caught up in his power.

She writhed as he pressed his face into her pubis. She moaned when his tongue lapped at the focus of her pleasure. "Please, Clay," she groaned.

Clay, kneeling between her legs, lifted her hips and entered her.

She gasped at the sensation. "Deeper," she said after a moment.

He thrust deeper and it felt wonderful. She'd been wanting this so long, wanting his body, wanting the sheer pleasure of the moment.

She wrapped her legs around his hips. Their bodies undulated. In moments she was at the brink. "Clay," she said breathlessly, her nails digging into his shoulders, "this feels so good."

They came together, their bodies heaving until they fell into stillness. Clay lay with his face pressed into her neck. She stroked his head, reveling in the crisp feel of his hair against her fingers. When he still did not move, she patted his butt. "Hey, cutie, you okay?"

He lifted his head and, looking into her eyes, sighed. "I'm beyond okay. Beyond...everything. How about you?"

"I'm fine. You kidding?"

He withdrew from her, moving to her side. But in spite of his words, she could tell by his voice there was something bothering him. "Hey, what's wrong?"

"As long as you're happy, that's all that matters."

"Clay?"

"Shh," he said, pressing his finger to her lips.

She was sure something was on his mind now. But how could she get him to tell her? Was it Laura? Had he thought of her? And was he sorry now they'd made love? "Tell me," she said. "Was it Laura? Do you feel like you betrayed her?"

Taking her fingers in his, he whispered, "No. I was only thinking of you. How much I want you." With that, he kissed her lower lip and gathered her closer. After a few minutes of silence, he said, "I'd like to make love with you again. If we only have tonight, then let's make the most of it."

She looked into his eyes, her heart raging in agreement, screaming yes. But in spite of his words, she could see in his eyes he was offering more than just this one night of love. She also knew she didn't want to resist.

And so they touched each other, quietly, gently at first, losing themselves in one another. The pleasure they felt was mixed with tenderness and caring, a pleasure that grew out of feeling for the person, a pleasure of sharing and giving. She felt it strongly. It terrified her, but once she was in its grip, she was lost.

Clay entered her and they lay entwined in each other's arms, kissing, caressing one another, embracing their feelings as well as each other. She gave herself up to him as she'd never given herself to any man. She made love with Clay McCormick until she was totally and completely lost in him, body and soul.

For a long time afterward, they lay holding each other, holding hands, fingers interlocked. They stared at the shadows dancing on the ceiling and Erica wondered how long this peace could last.

"This was special for you," she said, "wasn't it?"

"Yes. This is what I wanted."

"Since when? For how long?"

He hesitated before he said, "When you asked me what I was going to do with the ranch after I was gone. I thought about the children I didn't have. And the wife."

"That's the future," she said, her anxiety suddenly welling.

"Yes, but it reminded me how dead I was inside, how afraid. That knowledge made me want to feel, to love. I realized I wanted you, Erica. I followed my feelings and this is where they led me. Right here with you. And this is where I want to be…forever."

Forever. Couldn't he see that wasn't in the cards? Their love couldn't last forever—because forever didn't exist, not for her. But she didn't tell him that because she knew he didn't want to hear it. So instead she lay still for a long time, listening to the crackling fire. And then she heard his breathing deepen in sleep.

Erica sighed. She was glad they'd made love. Glad that Clay had been honest with her. But didn't he understand that she would never have children, that she'd be lucky to live a normal life expectancy? Didn't he see that making love, and falling in love, with someone like her couldn't work?

CLAY WAS AWAKENED by the warm rays of the sun angling in the window. Lord, he'd slept in. It had to be nine, maybe even ten. Checking his watch, he saw it was nine thirty-five. This hadn't happened since...well, a couple of years ago in Vegas, when he'd gotten so drunk he'd barely staggered to his room and hadn't woken up until eleven the next morning.

Erica was not beside him. Was she in the bathroom? Clay listened, but didn't hear any telltale sounds, like splashing water. He couldn't imagine her sitting in a cold tub. Besides, he'd have heard her lugging in the water. Maybe she was fiddling with her hair.

Clay yawned, amazed he'd slept so late. This time, it hadn't been drink. It had been something much better. Making love with a woman was the best sedative known to man. It was more than just the physical part, the release. It was surrendering to intimacy, the contentment of giving and receiving. He'd truly known that only once before in his life— with Laura. That alone said a great deal about his feelings for Erica.

He listened again, expecting to hear her rattling around in the cabin somewhere. But there was only silence. "Erica?" he called. "You in the bathroom?"

There was no answer. Had she gone outside? Maybe for a walk?

Clay got up from the pallet. The coals in the fireplace were still warm, but the fire had long since gone out. There was no glow of red, just chalky ash.

Standing before the fireplace, he dressed. His extra shirt—the one Erica had worn—was hanging on the chair. Her blouse was gone. She'd dressed. Mostly likely she'd gone for a walk. He went to the window and saw no sign of her out front. Going to the rear of the house, he couldn't see her there, either. Then it occurred to him she'd probably gone back to the ghost town to do some more work. He went to the bathroom and found she'd cleared out all her things. Lord, she must have been super quiet because he was normally a light sleeper.

After washing up, he returned to the main room, noticing for the first time she'd taken all her work materials with her. Yep, she was definitely working. He decided to saddle the horses and go find her. If she was really involved in what she was doing, he might even give her a little extra time, but they couldn't linger for long. They were expected back last night and Julia would worry.

Clay went out back and around the storage shed where he'd tethered the horses. The Appaloosa was gone. Looking inside the shed, he saw that the saddle and tack were gone, as well. He shook his head, amazed by her industriousness. How she'd managed to throw a saddle on that horse, much less know what to do once she had, he couldn't imagine. But she'd told him she was a quick study. Why she'd bothered, confounded him. She could have walked. A sense of independence, a desire to be self-sufficient—that's all he could figure.

He returned to the house to straighten up, put things away and lock up. It didn't take long. Back at

the shed, he saddled his horse, secured his saddlebags and headed to town. Coming around Boot Hill,
he saw no sign of either her or the Appaloosa. Clay
urged his horse into a trot, for the first time feeling
concern. He went to the saloon. She wasn't there. He
checked around back of both sides of the street. No
Erica, no horse. What the hell happened to her?
Could she have ridden off into the countryside a
ways? Maybe to get a picture of the town from a distance?

Feeling a sense of urgency, he went to the building where Erica had been on the roof and climbed
up the ladder. From there he surveyed the countryside. There was no sign of her anywhere. Then it
struck him that she'd returned to the ranch. But
why? If she hadn't felt well, surely she'd have awakened him. Could it have been she was running from
him?

Panic rose in his blood. He was concerned for her
safety, wary of her desperation, but most of all, fear-
ful of what she was thinking. His making love to her
must have upset her. What had he said that would
have driven her to run from him? Obviously he had
to find out.

Clay clambered down from the roof, mounted his
horse and took off down the road, headed for the
canyon. It was hard to tell how much of a head start
she had—an hour, or three or four. He wasn't particularly worried about her getting lost, but he was
concerned about her hurting herself. God only knew
how well she'd secured the saddle. If she hadn't
cinched it up properly, it could easily slip or even
fall off. It wasn't hard to imagine her lying along the

trail with a broken leg, broken ribs or another bump on her head.

He urged his horse into a gallop, hoping to catch her before disaster struck. He couldn't help thinking it would, because last night had been too good for some trouble not to come of it. He was seized by that old fear of being snake-bit. Again he wondered what he'd said and done. How could he have been so blind that he could make love with a woman and not realize she was upset?

Clay rode hard for the next hour and a half. He stopped once at a muddy creek bed and studied the tracks, deciding that a rider had passed by in the last few hours and it had to be Erica since there was no other likely candidate. He was relieved on two scores. First, he was glad she'd made it this far safely, and second, it was good to know he hadn't left her back at the town. He was still concerned, though, that she'd been upset enough to flee like this. There was a desperation in what she'd done and that really worried him.

CLAY ARRIVED at the ranch house after four hours of hard riding. As he'd come in, he'd seen the Appaloosa in the corral. There was no sign of Erica's car at the house. He rode right up to the front door, leaped off his horse and went inside.

"Gram?" he called, stomping through the house. "Gram? Where are you? Rosita? Where the hell is everybody?"

He found his grandmother in the sunroom, reading. She took off her glasses as he came in. For several moments they stared at each other.

"Where is she?" he finally said.

"Gone."

"Gone where?"

"Back to Denver."

Clay groaned, tossing his hat on the floor, putting his hands on his hips in frustration. "Why?"

"Maybe I should be asking *you* that, Clay."

"Well, didn't she say anything?"

"Just that she'd gathered all the information she needed and that she wanted to go home and work on her report. She said it was better if she wasn't around for a while."

"Better for who?"

"I didn't ask, but I gathered she meant better for herself, and maybe for you, as well. Whatever you did, Clay, it upset her."

"Damn," he said, kicking his foot at the air.

"I hope you didn't take advantage of her, Clay. A girl doesn't act this rashly unless she has a darn good reason."

"Gram, I didn't do a thing she didn't want to do herself," he said, wiping his sweaty forehead on his sleeve.

"Sometimes if things are vague…a man misinterprets," Julia said.

"Believe me, Erica's not shy about making her desires known. If I misinterpreted anything, it was how she felt, not what she wanted."

"Whatever it was you did, it certainly gave her a jolt."

"I reckon so." He slumped down on a straight chair near the entrance to the room.

"What are you going to do about it?" Julia asked.

"I'd like to make amends, but, to be honest, I'm

afraid of making things worse. Every damn thing I do with that woman seems to backfire."

"If she likes you, Clay, then your tactics are wrong. You can't disregard her feelings and her needs."

"Gram, what do you do when a woman's need is to be as far from you as possible?"

"What are you saying, that she's afraid?"

He sighed. "That's as good a way to put it as any, I guess."

"I don't know then," Julia said. "Ultimately all you can do is reassure her—assuming, of course, you can say the things she needs to hear."

"That right there is my problem, Gram. What she thinks she needs to hear is 'Goodbye, adios, see you around.' And those aren't words I'm hankering to say."

"I guess the only solution, then, is to find another way."

Clay got to his feet. "Sometimes I think a man's better off keeping company with a sidewinder," he said, stomping off.

"Clay, what are you going to do?"

He stopped at the door and looked back at her. "For starters, take a hot bath."

"And then?"

"Try to figure out what's in that woman's mind and what I should do about it."

"Want some advice?"

He gave another weary sigh. "Can't hurt."

"Tenderness. Compassion. Understanding."

"I thought that's what I was doing."

"Try again, Clay. Try again."

13

ERICA HAD BEEN at her computer off and on all day and she hadn't done three pages of quality work. All she could do was think about Clay. Why did he have to make love to her like that? Didn't he know that kind of love didn't last forever? Hadn't they both found that out the hard way?

They had both fallen into the trap of letting whatever happened happen. It was wrong to try to blame Clay. She'd put herself in the predicament out of weakness and that was the worst possible reason. The only relationships that worked were ones you entered out of conviction—everyone knew that. What she needed to do now was obvious. She had to climb back in the saddle and refuse to get down until she got where she was going. If she took anything from this experience, it had to be that.

Knowing there was no point in staring at her computer, she turned the damn thing off and put the dustcover over it—which brought to mind the dusty sheepskins on which she'd made love with Clay. How could the most beautiful night of her life also be the most traumatic?

During the long drive back to Denver she'd relived those moments, every second. Some recollections brought a smile to her face, others brought tears. There wasn't a thing about Clay McCormick she disliked, unless it was his stubbornness and the fact that he couldn't take no for an answer. Why couldn't he trust that she knew what she wanted? He was so sure he knew best, which was just like a man.

Erica had gone to her tiny kitchen and was peering into the refrigerator when her doorbell sounded. Glancing at the clock, she went to the front door and looked through the peephole. It was Sally. Erica opened the door.

"I know I'm early," Sally Nobel said, "but the boss freed me after my last project and I thought why not come straight over instead of going home? Might as well help you with dinner." Pushing a blond curl back off her face, she smiled. "And I bought a chocolate cake at the bakery, your favorite." She held up the box.

"Sally, you're a godsend," Erica said, embracing her.

Sally was several inches shorter and the same age. They'd been almost like sisters for years, having known each other since high school. Erica had called her the previous evening from Vail, where she'd stopped for dinner. They hadn't talked for long, but enough for Sally to realize she was suffering.

"Why not come straight to my place?" her friend had said.

But Erica knew it would be a night for crying and she wanted to be alone. "No, I won't be getting in until late. Why don't you come over for dinner tomorrow night? I'll make chicken Marengo."

That's what they'd agreed to do.

Sally put her purse on the antique sideboard that Erica had bought at a flea market with the fat bonus she'd gotten from her first consulting job. Then both women headed for the kitchen.

"I've still got that wine you drank the last time you were here," Erica said, opening the door of the fridge and peering in. "Can I pour you a glass?"

"Sure, I could use it," Sally said, putting the cake box on the counter. "But then, I imagine you could as well."

"Actually, yes. But there are quicker ways to kill myself, so I'll pass."

Sally sat at the tiny table as Erica poured the wine. She waited until Erica handed her the glass. "So, let's have it," she said. "How did the cowboy break your heart?"

Erica pulled up the other chair and sat, feeling dreadfully tired, more fatigued than she had after all the horseback riding, lovemaking and driving. "By loving me a little too much."

Sally tried not to smile but Erica saw her lips twitch anyway. "Odd problem," her friend said simply.

"You know I can't afford to get involved with anyone. It's just not in the cards."

"And he wanted a relationship?" Sally said, taking a sip of wine.

"He wasn't interested in just sex. He made love with me. And I think he's more than halfway in love with me."

"I think that's sweet."

"It's sweet, all right. You can't believe how innocent he is. I mean he's a macho, tough, strong man of the earth, yet in many ways pure as the driven snow."

"What do you mean?"

"I mean emotionally. I can tell he thinks he loves me."

"*Thinks* he loves you?"

"Sally, he hasn't been involved with anyone in years, not since his fiancée died of cancer. It's like he came out of hibernation and saw me standing there, a woman with hepatitis C. That's the worst possible thing that could happen."

Sally looked down at her nails. "To him or to you?"

"Him. Well…me, too. To both of us, actually."

"So he likes you and you like him. Your classical American tragedy."

"But I'm not just anyone! And neither is Clay!"

"No, you're people with problems who just might be able to help each other."

"Hey," Erica protested, "whose side are you on, anyway?"

Sally sipped some more wine. "Actually, I'm trying to understand the problem."

"The problem is, I don't need the disappointment, the pain, the heartache. And he doesn't either, Sally. I'd be kidding myself if I didn't recognize that. Look what happened with Tom."

"If I'm not mistaken, Tom dumped you."

"Clay has even more reason."

"So kick him in the stomach before he can kick you."

Erica got up abruptly and went to the refrigerator. "You're trying to talk me out of my feelings, Sally, and that's not helpful."

"I'm not trying to talk you out of anything. I'm trying to help you see what you're really saying. I think you're afraid. You were hurt in the past and you don't want it to happen again."

"Maybe so, but I know for a fact I can't get emotionally involved with anyone."

"You can't get emotionally involved with anyone who can't handle it," Sally retorted.

"Believe me, Clay McCormick is the last man on earth who could handle a thing like this, and I think deep down he knows it."

There was a knock at the door and both Erica and Sally turned.

Erica headed for the front room. It was probably her neighbor, Mrs. Martin, who saved the mail for her when she went on short trips.

She peered through the peephole and saw a man in a cowboy hat. Clay! Turning, she fell back against the door, her hands to her mouth. Sally stood at the kitchen door, staring at her, a questioning look on her face.

"It's him," she whispered as there was another knock, this one louder than before.

"You might as well open the door," Sally said. "It doesn't sound like he's going to go away anytime soon."

Erica looked down at herself. She was in shorts and a T-shirt, her hair pulled back behind her ears. No makeup to speak of. What better proof was there that she wasn't expecting this? Sally was right, though, she had to let him in. Erica took a deep breath and pulled the door open.

His expression was not exactly grim, but he wasn't smiling either. There was a glimmer of friendliness in his eye, but only a glimmer.

"Couldn't you have left me a note?" he said without introduction.

"I didn't know what to say."

"'I wasn't captured by a band of renegades, but am returning to the ranch of my own free will,' would have been a start."

"I'm sorry, Clay, but I felt a terrible need to get out of there. I guess I was feeling desperate."

"Can we talk about it?"

Erica glanced back at Sally, who was still at the kitchen door. Clay only then noticed her.

"I didn't realize you had company," he said.

After an awkward moment, Sally came to the door. "Hi," she said, extending her hand, "I'm Erica's friend, Sally Nobel."

He removed his hat as he took her hand. "Clay McCormick, ma'am."

"I've heard a lot about you, Clay," she said.

"Really, ma'am?"

"Women love to talk about men," Sally said. "But I'm sure that doesn't come as a surprise. Come in. If Erica wasn't in a state of shock, I'm sure she'd invite you herself."

Clay looked at her. Erica nodded. "I guess I am in a state of shock. Please, do come in."

He stepped inside and she closed the door. She felt weak, light-headed, disoriented. Clay McCormick in her apartment was about as incongruous as it could get. This was fantasy intruding on reality.

The three of them stood in the small room, Clay looking as uncomfortable as she felt. Once again, Sally jumped into the breach.

"You know what, Erica? I didn't pick up any vanilla ice cream to go with that cake. I was going to do it on the way over and forgot all about it. I'll just run up to the supermarket and grab a pint."

"No, don't leave, Sally. I've got ice cream in the freezer."

"Ah, but not my favorite flavor. It's got to be gourmet French vanilla with this cake. Do you like chocolate cake and ice cream, Clay? If you're staying for dinner, I'll get enough for all three of us. Maybe I should get a quart." Sally got her purse from the sideboard. "I shouldn't be more than half an hour or so." She went to the door. After opening it, she hesitated. "Or would you rather we have our dinner tomorrow night, Erica?" she asked. "I imagine you and Clay have a lot to discuss. And I had a really early morning. Maybe it would be better to put it off. Why don't I give you a call tomorrow?"

"I don't mean to interrupt your evening, ma'am," Clay said. "You and Erica had plans and I'm intruding."

"Think nothing of it. We can have dinner anytime," Sally said, looking at Erica for signals. "I'm so tired I wouldn't be much company." She hesitated only the briefest moment before giving Erica a knowing smile. "Well, goodbye. Hope to see you again, Clay." The door closed and she was gone.

Erica would have stopped her because she really didn't want to be alone with Clay, but at the same time she knew he couldn't say whatever it was that brought him here with anyone else around. Maybe it was best to get it over with. She looked at him from the corner of her eye, gesturing toward the white duck sofa. She took the navy chintz armchair her aunt and uncle had given her when they refurnished their house.

"Nice little place you've got here," he said, looking around.

Erica knew it was nothing special. She hadn't spent much money on either the furniture or the furnishings. She had a few cute things and a few things with sentimental value, but the apartment was far from elegant. "Thanks, Clay."

Their eyes met. His expression was a little closer to a smile but there was also pain there.

"Look," she said, "I'm really sorry I ran off that way, but the truth is I couldn't face you."

"How did I offend you? Do you mind telling me that?"

"You didn't offend me at all."

He contemplated that. "It would have been better, I take it, if we hadn't made love? Our feelings were just a little too strong."

She lowered her eyes. "I didn't want to care for you too much, Clay, and I was in danger of letting that happen."

"What exactly were you afraid of?" he asked.

She folded her hands and pressed them to her mouth, searching for a way to express herself. This was so hard. How did you tell a person you didn't want to love them because it was too painful?

"Look," he said, "I know your illness is an issue for you. Ever since you told me about the hepatitis, I've been tiptoeing around it. I reckon maybe the time has come for a little more honesty and a little less diplomacy.

"Erica, I know we've only known each other for a short time and we have a lot of getting acquainted to do. But damn it, I care about you. And I think you feel the same way. We owe it to each other and to ourselves to check this thing out."

"What's to check out?" she asked. "We know we're attracted to each other. But so what? What's attraction? Hell, what's love? We still have to face reality, and reality is that I could die at any time. Reality is that you have your ranch, your life and I have mine. Don't you see, we've got no future? You need a wife and children. I can't have children. It would be too risky. You need a normal life."

"You think I've got a normal life now?"

"You could."

"Erica, you're the first woman I've given a hoot about since Laura. Don't you think that makes you kind of special? Do you think I can turn my back on someone because they've got some virus and they don't consider raising cattle the most important thing in life? I'm not that shallow, Erica, nor that callous."

"Of course not. I didn't mean to imply—"

"Sweetheart, did I ever tell you what rule number one of the Cowboy Code is?"

She shook her head.

"'When you find the woman of your dreams, *never, ever* let her go!'" He leaned forward, grabbed her hand and pulled her close. "You're the most wonderful, sweet, lovely, intelligent, feisty woman I've ever known. Not only that, you can saddle a horse. How in tarnation could I live with myself if I let you get away?"

She turned her face into his shoulder and sobbed quietly. Clay rubbed her back. The crying grew harder, her body shaking. "Clay, you're making it so difficult," she murmured. "What if I get sick?"

"Hey," he said, making her look at him, "there are no guarantees in life. We both know that. There's not an awful lot we can do to control the future, but we can take the opportunities that are given to us. You know who taught me that?"

She shook her head.

"You did, Erica. You!" He took a handkerchief from his pocket, and handed it to her. "Until you came along, I'd shut out life. I buried myself in that ranch of mine. Sure, I love the place, but until I met you, I'd been denying myself all the other possibilities. I denied myself the opportunity for love."

"It doesn't have to be me," she said, wiping her eyes with the handkerchief.

"You're right. It could be somebody else. Another month and you and I might be wondering what the heck we saw in each other, but we'll never know unless we try. Anyway, I've got a hunch you're meant to be my woman, sweetheart."

"A hunch?"

He smiled. "Well, maybe it's more than a hunch. Yesterday I went into town and I stopped by the feed store. Sure enough, Alma Jones grabbed my hand again. Erica, she said you were the one."

"You came to Denver to see me because of some old lady who thinks she's a fortune-teller?"

"Nope. I came to Denver because of the way I feel about you. If you want to know what finally tipped the scales, it was when you slipped out of the guest house, saddled up that Appaloosa and rode back to the house without me so much as realizing it."

"Oh, really. And what if Alma had told you to forget me?"

"I'd have come here anyway. After all, no cowboy in his right mind believes in fortune-telling."

Erica put her arms around his neck and hugged him. Clay held her tight, kissing her tear-streaked face. She kissed him back.

"Clay, you're the sweetest man I've ever known, but there's not a practical bone in your body—at least when it comes to love. You're caught up in the emotion of the moment. What if I die?"

"Then I'll have the best hours, days, months, years of my life between now and then." He kissed her cheek.

"I'm not a cowgirl," she said. "Your life is not my life."

"You know, it wasn't Gram's life either. But she's lived there happily for more than fifty years because of two things—she loved my grandfather and he was smart enough to encourage her to lead her own life. She had the Cowboy Club. You can be a consultant or anything else you wish. All I'm asking is that you share your life with me, the same way I'm willing to share mine with you."

She bit her lip, too choked up to respond. This was much too good to be true.

"Come on, what do you say? All I'm asking, sweetheart, is that you come back to Red Rock with me and give it a try. You've got a project to finish and I've got a ranch to run. I bet if we try real hard we can find a little time for each other. I don't know about you, but I'd kinda like to see if reality can live up to the dreams I have for us."

She kissed him then, kissed him deeply, letting

that be her answer. She didn't want to say the words out loud yet, but in her heart of hearts she already knew that, for her, Clay McCormick was a dream come true.

_____ Epilogue _____

THE LIGHTS WENT DOWN and so did the crowd noise. A hush came over the Cowboy Club, the only sounds the faint clatter of dishes coming from the kitchen. Then a spot came on the stage and Julia Sommers stood there in a slinky, high-necked, long-sleeve dress, a microphone in her hand. There was immediate applause and cheers and cries of "Julia! Julia!"

Erica snuggled closer to Clay in the booth, grasping his arm with both her hands. She could feel the excitement in the air. As the noise died down, Julia looked out at the crowd, her eyes glistening.

"Autumn," she said. "This is a busy time of year in this part of the country. The ranchers are bringing cattle down from the high country. Before we know it, there'll be snow on the mountain peaks. We've seen it all before, yet this year is different, because this autumn Cody James passed on.

"Cody's death means the loss of a dear friend for me, and also for all of you. And tonight we are going to celebrate Cody's life. I say celebrate because Cody didn't want long faces at his wake. He wanted a party and so here we are, having a party in remembrance of one of the best-loved figures in Red Rock.

"The letter of instructions Cody left concerning tonight specified I was to sing, if I was able. Well,

Cody, I'm not particularly able, but I'm going to give it a try for you anyway, old buddy."

There was applause. In their dark corner booth, Clay patted Erica's hand and kissed her hair.

"But before I do my song, I'd like to share some happy news. I know that's what Cody would have wanted. As to the future of the Cowboy Club, Dax Charboneau asked me to assure you that the club will continue as it has in the past."

Another cheer.

"For those of you who haven't heard, Cody's interest in the club is now in the hands of his niece, a young lady from New York named Chloe James. Dax has been in communication with her and he assures me that an arrangement is being worked out that will keep things just as we all want them."

Applause and whistles.

"Now, on a more personal note, I'd like to share a little joy that has come into my own life. Most of you are aware that I've been wanting to turn that old movie ghost town I own into a theme park. My grandson, Clay McCormick, and I have had discussions about that in the past..."

A few hoots of laughter.

"Well, I'm pleased to tell you that I've recently received a feasibility study on the project from my consultant, which is most encouraging. Just as important, Clay and I have worked out an arrangement for access to the site. So, if I get the financial backing, and receive all the required permits as expected, we could be breaking ground as early as next spring. That means a lot of tourist dollars and jobs for the citizens of Red Rock."

Cheers and foot stamping.

"One last, related piece of news and a particular source of joy to me. Those of you who know Clay, and most of you do, know him to be a dyed-in-the-wool rancher, and man of the land in the truest and best sense. Well, I've gotta tell you, something has recently come into Clay's life that has taken some of his attention away from his ranch. And that something is a woman."

Clay put his arm around Erica as the crowd hooted and whistled and stamped their feet approvingly.

"Last Sunday, Clay McCormick became engaged to marry Miss Erica Ross, lately of Denver, soon to be not only Clay's wife, but also the project manager of my theme park." Throwing back her head and laughing, Julia added, "Can you imagine a more unlikely pair? Fellas, if you don't know already, therein lies the power of a woman!"

People laughed and applauded, and there were cries of "Right on!" from a few females in the audience. At the same time, the spot swung to the corner booth, bathing Clay and Erica in light. In response to the cheers, Clay got to his feet.

Clearing his throat, he said, "I reckon a fella can't rightly let remarks like that pass without comment." Then, looking down at Erica, he went on, "Anybody who lays eyes on this angel sitting beside me can understand how anything could come between me and my ranch."

There were oohs and aahs as Clay kissed her hand. Erica looked up at him with glistening eyes, her heart swelling with joy.

"Which is not to say my ranching days are over, by any means," he added. "Erica and I have agreed to build a life together and the Lone Eagle and Gram's ghost town will be a big part of it. The wedding, incidentally, will be at the community church with a reception here at the Cowboy Club to follow. And you're all invited!"

There were more cheers, then some of the women started chanting, "The ring, the ring, let's see the ring!"

Blushing, Erica held up her hand so that her two-carat diamond sparkled in the spotlight. Sounds of approval came from the audience. The spot swung back to Julia.

"And now friends, without further ado, I'd like to sing a special favorite of mine and one Cody was always partial to, 'Moon River,' especially dedicated tonight to Clay and Erica."

The pianist behind her played a few introductory bars, then Julia launched into a mellow rendition of the song. Erica listened with tears in her eyes, so happy she could burst.

It had been a remarkable few months, one of those periods in which the course of her life had changed forever. She and Clay had talked about it over the weeks as their love had deepened. The future was uncertain, but their love was definite. No matter what fate had in store for them, they would always have their love.

The Sunday before, they'd sat in the same corner booth of the Cowboy Club where Hap Sommers had proposed to Julia all those years ago. There, Clay had told Erica that they had to cherish their days together above all else because when all was said and done, their time together was their most valuable possession. And then, with a tear in his eye, he had slipped the diamond on her finger and peered deeply into her eyes, asking to marry her.

Erica had said simply, "Yes. I'll marry you. And I'll love you forever."

"Is that a promise?" he'd asked, kissing her hand.

"You bet, Mr. McCormick. And in case you haven't heard, it's rule number one in the Cowgirl Code. 'If you find the cowboy of your dreams, grab him, hold on tight and love him forever. Because if you do, all your dreams will come true and you'll live happily ever after.'"

DAX CHARBONEAU downed his whiskey, neat, and checked his watch for the third time in as many minutes. He was in his office at the Cowboy Club, sitting in the very chair Cody James had occupied forever. He was trying to decide if he'd been set up by his friends, or if he was about to meet the real Miss Chloe James.

Heath had called over an hour ago saying that the lady was on her way into town, and that he'd seen her out on the old cutoff road. Dax had asked Heath how he knew it was her, what she looked like, what her mood and demeanor were. But Heath had refused to say another word. Said he'd done the neighborly thing by warning him, and then he'd hung up.

Dax could have killed him.

For a while after the call, he'd been sure that Heath had been putting him on. After all, when he'd spoken to Cody's niece on the phone last week, she hadn't sounded at all enthusiastic about the notion of coming to Red Rock. To the contrary, she had wanted him to make her an offer over the phone! And when he told her in no uncertain terms that he didn't do business that way she'd seemed sort of…well, put out.

Had something changed her mind? Was Miss

Chloe James, big-time shoe designer lady from New York City, actually on her way to Red Rock, or was Heath putting him on? Dax could imagine the boys hiring some obnoxious female to come to the club and make a scene—embarrass the hell out of him— all in the name of fun.

Dax picked up his whiskey and finished the last drop that was in the glass. He'd been thinking about the club the past few weeks, the things he wanted to do when—or, maybe *if*—he gained control. Having Cody as a partner had been a blessing. Dax had learned a lot from the old boy.

Just then there was a knock at the door.

"Yo," he said.

The door opened. It was the club's long-time hostess, Wanda Ramirez. Wanda was in her early fifties, plump, with big white hair and fake eyelashes as black as coal. Her usual attire was a lacy white off-the-shoulder peasant blouse and Mexican skirt.

"There's a lady to see you out front, sugar," she said.

"Does she have a name?"

"She says it's Chloe James," Wanda replied, arching a brow.

"And?"

"Well, you'd better come see for yourself."

Dax got up from the worn desk that had been in this office about as long as the place had had a roof. "Should I comb my hair first?" he joked to Wanda as he stepped around it.

"Don't reckon it's necessary in this case, sugar."

Dax smiled. His buddies *had* prepared a prank. Either that or Miss Chloe James was completely disreputable. When he got to the door, he stopped. "Are Heath and Ford and the other boys out there?"

"Most of 'em. Why?"

"Nothing, I was just curious," he said. "Look, will you tell Miss James I'll be a minute? I want to grab my files."

Wanda left and Dax went to the file cabinet. He wasn't really going to do business with whoever it was out there, but he was determined to be professional and not bat an eye, regardless how she looked or what she did.

He took his time with the files, figuring it'd be a good thing to let her cool her heels for a while. Finally, Dax smoothed the collar of his black shirt, centered his silver buckle, picked up his stack of files and opened the door. He walked along the short hall and out the door that accessed the club.

Dax stopped to appraise the scene. He saw his friends at the bar, near the dance floor. Sliding his eyes over, he saw the woman they were discreetly watching.

She was pacing back and forth just at the corner of the dance floor, her purse on the table at the nearest booth, her arms folded over her chest. Dax's mouthed sagged open.

She was stunningly attractive—he noticed that immediately—but she looked as though she'd run into trouble. Or a buzz saw. First, her jacket was torn at the sleeve and there was a big smudge of something on her cheek, grease, maybe. As she turned sharply with the flair of a fashion model with an attitude, Dax noticed the kick pleat in her skirt was torn clear to the top of her thigh, revealing the sexiest leg he'd seen in an age. Best of all, perhaps, were her ankles, so slim the finest racehorse would be envious, especially in light of the red ankle straps on the very sexy and very high heels on her feet. He could only stare.

Just then she caught sight of him and stopped dead in her tracks. Was there fury in her eyes, or simple impatience? he wondered. Could this be the *real* Chloe James?

Dax glanced over at the boys, all of whom were eagerly watching. It was a set-up, he was sure. Even so, he could hardly take his eyes off the woman. She cocked her head inquisitively as if to say "Well, are *you* Dax Charboneau? And if so, why are you just standing there?" Gathering himself, Dax made his way toward the dance floor, taking in the pleasing lines of her body as he approached. Whatever the hell was going on, he liked what he saw.

The woman moved toward him, her expression no-nonsense. "Mr. Charboneau?"

"Miss James?"

She thrust her hand toward him. As he switched the stack of files to his other hand, her heel caught on the edge of the dance floor and she came flying at him like a missile. Somehow he managed to catch her, but the files went sailing from his hand.

Dax heard the files land on the floor with a splat, but he didn't so much as turn his head to see if the papers had flown out of them because Chloe James—or whoever she was—was staring up at him, her huge emerald eyes round as saucers. Dax held her by the waist and shoulder and she lay back, as though they'd been slow dancing and he'd dipped her. Pulling himself together as he gazed into her eyes, he gave her his most wicked sexy smile.

"Welcome to the Cowboy Club, Miss James. I've been expecting you."

Look for
#714 THE BRIDE WORE BOOTS
by Janice Kaiser,
available in January 1999!

HARLEQUIN®
Temptation

He's strong. He's sexy.
He's up for grabs!

Harlequin Temptation and
Texas Men magazine present:

1998 Mail Order Men

#691 THE LONE WOLF
by Sandy Steen—July 1998

#695 SINGLE IN THE SADDLE
by Vicki Lewis Thompson—August 1998

#699 SINGLE SHERIFF SEEKS...
by Jo Leigh—September 1998

#703 STILL HITCHED, COWBOY
by Leandra Logan—October 1998

#707 TALL, DARK AND RECKLESS
by Lyn Ellis—November 1998

#711 MR. DECEMBER
by Heather MacAllister—December 1998

Mail Order Men—
Satisfaction Guaranteed!

Available wherever Harlequin books are sold.

HARLEQUIN®
Makes any time special ™

Look us up on-line at: http://www.romance.net   HTEMOM

Take 2 bestselling love stories FREE

Plus get a FREE surprise gift!

Special Limited-Time Offer

Mail to Harlequin Reader Service®

3010 Walden Avenue
P.O. Box 1867
Buffalo, N.Y. 14240-1867

YES! Please send me 2 free Harlequin Temptation® novels and my free surprise gift. Then send me 4 brand-new novels every month, which I will receive before they appear in bookstores. Bill me at the low price of $3.12 each plus 25¢ delivery and applicable sales tax, if any.* That's the complete price, and a saving of over 10% off the cover prices—quite a bargain! I understand that accepting the books and gift places me under no obligation ever to buy any books. I can always return a shipment and cancel at any time. Even if I never buy another book from Harlequin, the 2 free books and the surprise gift are mine to keep forever.

142 HEN CH7G

Name	(PLEASE PRINT)	
Address	Apt. No.	
City	State	Zip

This offer is limited to one order per household and not valid to present Harlequin Temptation® subscribers. *Terms and prices are subject to change without notice. Sales tax applicable in N.Y.

UTEMP-98

©1990 Harlequin Enterprises Limited

COMING NEXT MONTH

#705 BODY LANGUAGE Margaret Brownley
Hero for Hire

Rick Westley was convinced the letter bomb that destroyed his office was a fluke. Who'd want to hurt *him?* But after spending a few days with Jacquie (Jack) Summers "protecting" him, he suspected someone *was* out to get him…and that someone was his sexy yet accident-prone bodyguard.

#706 THE ADVENTUROUS BRIDE Molly Liholm

Megan Cooper was surprised—and delighted—when sexy, rugged Adam Smith broke in to her bookstore and held her hostage. Before she knew it, he'd stolen her heart. Before *he* knew it, Meg was helping his investigation—and tempting him with her passion. Now Adam was the one in danger…of falling in love.

#707 TALL, DARK AND RECKLESS Lyn Ellis
Mail Order Men

Lone Star Lover? Texas Ranger Matt Travis thrived on taking risks, on encountering the unexpected—until he found himself corralled by a throng of sex-starved women! Worse, gorgeous TV newscaster Dee Cates seemed to be enjoying his predicament. And suddenly Matt was tempted to live up to his reputation.…

#708 FLIRTING WITH DANGER Jamie Denton
Blaze

Tough cop Mason O'Neill figured he'd seen it all. Clearly gorgeous, sexy Bailey Grayson was out of her element on the streets of L.A. He arrested her to keep her safe. But who would protect Bailey from him…and his burning desire for her?
